WITTGENSTEIN
and the
GOSHAWK

WITTGENSTEIN
and the
GOSHAWK
A fable

Patrick Watson

McArthur & Company
Toronto

First Published in Canada in 2004 by
McArthur & Company
322 King Street West, Suite 402
Toronto, Ontario
M5V 1J2
www.mcarthur-co.com

Library and Archives Canada Cataloguing in Publication

Watson, Patrick, 1929-
    Wittgenstein and the goshawk : a fable / Patrick Watson.

ISBN 1-55278-449-5

    I. Title.

PS8595.A85W58 2004   C813'.54   C2004-904191-6

The publisher would like to acknowledge the financial support of
the Government of Canada through the Book Publishing Industry
Development Program, The Canada Council for the Arts, and the
Ontario Arts Council for our publishing activities. We also acknowledge the Government of Ontario through the Ontario Media Development Corporation Ontario Book Initiative.

Illustrations by Pat Lyons
Design and Composition by Michael P.M. Callaghan
Printed in Canada by Friesens

10 9 8 7 6 5 4 3 2 1

Chapter One

Astur

Waboosh the big rabbit might have been all right if she had not moved. Her fur was the same colour as the snowy open patch of forest floor she had been crossing when she sensed the presence of danger, and froze. If she had stayed still like that she would have been invisible.

The goshawk, Astur the Magnificent, was perched on a dead branch at house height above the edge of the little clearing. She had been looking the other way, scanning the deep woods to the north of the clearing, when a soft sound — the snowshoe rabbit's hop into the open just behind her — caused her to turn slowly and majestically and with dignity, as always, towards the sound. Perhaps the rabbit had caught that slow head movement out of the corner of her big soft eyes. The hawk was otherwise perfectly still as she sat on the naked branch.

It was April snow, the last of the season, and only in the woods now. On the open ground the sun had melted it all. But on the flat white surface of this shaded clearing, tumbled with a few heavy lumps that had fallen from pine branches in the morning wind, the snowshoe rabbit in its winter coat, frozen as its instincts told it to be, looked like just another lump of that April snow.

Astur was hungry, *really* hungry. She had not eaten all day. Trailing from each of her ribbed yellow feet was a faded, slightly tattered leather strip, called a jess. There had once been tiny ball-shaped Pakistani soft steel bells attached to these jesses, but they had rusted and fallen off a long time ago. Her powerful eyes scanned below her, sweep, sweep. And then, when she puffed her feathers and raised her crest to stretch the wing muscles a little, stiff from sitting on that perch for several hours, the lump of snow down below her lost its nerve. Where there had been nothing but smooth snow in the open clearing, with those lumps around the edge fallen from branches above, now one of the lumps had shifted, and there appeared on the flat surface of the clearing a series of little dots, like colons accelerating across a page

::: : : : : : : : : : :

Dinner! Now it was the goshawk who froze, waiting for the perfect moment. The dots multiplied rapidly; the spaces between them got longer. Now Astur could see the shadow and then the shape of the terrified rabbit, leaping for its life, *thump, thump* towards the safety of the brambles on the far side of the clearing. For a moment the rabbit was out of sight behind the trunk of a pine as she entered the thick forest again. That was the time to strike, when the tree trunk would mask the first rush of the assassin from above. The wings thrust back as they drove the bird down faster than a stone would fall, a hundred miles an hour, then a hundred and fifty, the gap between the curved steel of her beak and that pine trunk closing fast.

Not fast enough. The rabbit came out beyond the pine just before the hawk cleared the trunk. She saw the hurtling shadow, gave an extra heart-stretching pump of her big hind feet and plunged into the brambles, feinting left, then right, into the tangle of growth. The hunter above was not to be shaken. She flew into the woods after her prey. Her senses guiding her past every shadow and flick of branch, she banked hard at every turn, tracking her prey with confidence, even though the trembling mammal was out of sight beneath brush at least half the time.

The forest closed in around the hawk. Tree trunks rippled through her side vision like fence rails. She skimmed just off the ground, looking for the opportunity to pounce and grasp with her scimitar talons the instant her prey came clear of cover. Shadows and solid things sped by in a blur. The trees were now too thick for flying. She put out her landing gear and hit the ground running, dodging left when the rabbit went right, right when it went left, closing, closing, one metre, half, ten centimetres.

But then the rabbit's pounding hind feet threw up a snowball that caught the goshawk right in the eyes. For a moment she was blinded. But she heard and sensed the terrified mammal right in front of her, pushed with her wings, struck with her feet, and sank the needle-sharp talons into the rabbit's haunches.

Mistake. The only way a goshawk weighing about one kilogram can safely take a hare three times her weight is to sink the claws of one foot into the head or the neck just below the head, the others into the loin or hindquarters, and instantly immobilize the victim. Astur had done it hundreds of times, six hundred, eight, perhaps more than a thousand. She knew her craft. But this time, momentarily blinded, she had just lashed out, and that proved a mistake.

Waboosh the snowshoe rabbit is properly known as the varying hare, and like all the hares her hind feet are a champion boxer's fists or a pair of small but cunning sledgehammers. Waboosh knew she had only about two seconds and she gave it everything she had. Those leather-shod pounders whammed up into the hawk's chest, and with a second smack the left uppercut got the bird hard on the side of the head, *whap* this way, *whap* that way, and knocked her cold. The hawk went down like a ton of feathers.

Which is, after all, just as heavy as a ton of bricks, when you think about it.

The rabbit was safe, gone, vanished into a burrow somewhere.

The hungry hawk shook the snow from her eyes, and tried to clear the pain and the blur from the blow to her head. It was outrageous. She, Astur of Russia, pride of the Court of St. Petersburg, sometime Sovereign Hawk Mascot of the Imperial Military Academy, had been humiliated by a . . . by a snowshoe rabbit! Well, a hare, to be accurate, but still.

Astur, the Royal Hawk, late of the Imperial Court, ten years flying and hunting professionally for His Royal Eminence Prince Vasily Voyeikoff, spat snow out of her beak, cleared her throat regally, and said just one word: "*Merde!*"

Now *merde* is a word that in French sounds not much ruder than "Darn it!" Or perhaps "Gosh darn it!" However, translated into English it is a pretty rude word, so we'll leave it in French. Which was the official language of the Court of Russia when Astur was flying and hunting there for the Prince. That's why she spoke French, very good French too, and why she looked down upon anyone who preferred anything less elegant such as English or Ojibwa. Or even Russian, which the Russian nobility rather despised.

For a fleeting moment Astur wondered if she were losing her touch. This is not the kind of thought a royal Russian raptor usually permits herself (for hawks are raptors too, it's not just dinosaurs and basketball players).

Astur gave three sweeping strokes of her long sails, and in one second was back on her branch over the tangled forest floor, still scanning for that, that @*&$% rabbit.

The wise rabbit never appeared.

Astur sighed. She thought about an open hayfield she had once hunted in the fall, on the edge of the wilderness park, an hour's flight away. She did not like to be out in the open, away from the forest. Flying with her prince, she had been given plenty of experience of the open field and the tasty food to be had there. But all her instincts were against it. She is a forest bird, the goshawk. That is where she belongs.

And yet . . . The field would be an easy hunt where she could at least count on a few mice: not really a substantial meal, but better than nothing. Or perhaps a squirrel — nasty dirty hairy things, you had to watch out for their bite, they were very quick even after you sank your claws in them. Small as they were, they gave you a lot of extra hairballs or castings to bring up afterwards, and heartburn too. But then, they were more substantial than mousemeat. She sighed, roused, opened her wings, took off gracefully but sadly, and headed for the hayfield. Spring would be here soon, with the grouse and the new young rabbits, and the mallards coming back from their migration. So for now she might as well get something to eat in the field, and then come back into the deep woods to roost for the night. And then she would dream of St. Petersburg.

Vasily Ilyich, third of the name, Prince of the House of Voyeikoff, was by 1917 almost penniless because of his father's fondness for the card table. The father's last extravagance had been to buy a goshawk as a tenth birthday present for young Prince Vasily. That was years ago. He could never afford another one. They had smuggled Astur in from Vienna where she had been poached in the famous Vienna Woods while she was still a tiny ball of fluff in the nest. Duke Ilya, the father, loved falconry almost as much as he loved cards; so he decided to give young Vasily a thorough training in the exacting craft of raising and hunting with birds of prey.

The goshawk became the one thing besides his title and his mother the Princess that Vasily really loved in life. And so, when they came and said that awful day, smoke rising all over St. Petersburg, and gunfire (and crowds of disgusting people in *working* clothes!) and soldiers deserting from the Imperial Army!

When they came and said that, yes, it really was a Revolution to overthrow the Czar, some disreputable agitator named Lenin, and there was still time to get away, Vasily grabbed a few gold British sovereigns wrapped in a peregrine falcon's ornamental leather hood, and Astur herself, and ran for it. The hawk, her more than a metre of wingspread folded grumpily as she sat on an ornamental perch of very bad taste, was disguised. That is, her cage was covered in an ornamental cloth that showed a name, the French equivalent of Polly, in gold embroidery all around its fringed bottom.

By the time the young Prince got off the boat in New York the gold sovereigns, many thousands of dollars' worth, were almost gone. But Astur had been well fed and groomed all the way across, and she had been much admired by the other passengers as Vasily, walking on the afterdeck, flew her from the fist for raw strips of filet mignon on a makeshift lure.

"My friend the Major General, Sascha, Count Ivanov, is in the hotel business in New York," the Prince told the other passengers. "Perhaps you are having heard of the famous Waldorf-Astoria Hotel? He is very well known amongst the finest families of New York and I am sure he will help me to recapturing my graceful way of life, as a true comrade. Well, as a brother; I should not using that terrible word 'comrade.'"

"But you seem so, well, so *young*, Your Highness," said a Mrs. Vanderbilt, who lived in New York, and was imagining that it might be quite splendid to give a Russian Imperial party some grand evening, and spring a surprise guest on some of her snooty friends. Wouldn't Mrs. J.P. Morgan just have a fit! "I mean so young to be going off on your own, like that. With no one to look after you. No family, no friends. Except, of course, for Count, what? Was it Ivanov? Perhaps he would like to come to the party too? Oh dear, I didn't mean to mention that yet, the party. But yes, you are very young."

The handsome Prince drew himself up, took a monocle from his breast pocket and used it to give himself an air of seriousness as he examined Mrs. Vanderbilt. Although he was vain, he had a serious and a thoughtful side too.

"I am almost twenty years old, Madame. Wolfgang Amadeus Mozart had written seventeen symphonya and twenty-eight concertya by the time he was twenty. Our dear Lord Jesus Christ was setting out to be redeeming the sinful world when He was my age. I am Scion of the House of Voyeikoff, a Master of the Hawks, Royal Class, one of only three in Eastern Europe and, I am told, shall to be the only one in all of America. And I am speaking five languages!"

By now the Prince had polished up his English enough to get by, having been informed before leaving Russia that they do not much like to speak French in New York.

*S*quinting against the bright sunlight, Vasily Ilyich, Prince Voyeikoff, walked through the bustle of Fifth Avenue, towards the corner of 35th Street and the Waldorf-Astoria Hotel, on whose elegant letterhead he had received two communiqués from his friend Major General Sascha the Count.

Some distance before reaching the hotel, he saw that there was a very grand military officer, by his splendid uniform, a General almost certainly, if not a Field Marshal, standing on the pavement in front of the main doors. This elegantly uniformed man was graciously nodding to lesser people who entered the hotel, once even holding the door open for a lady with what appeared to be a fox wrapped around her shoulders. She cannot be an aristocratic lady herself, Prince Vasily mused; she was actually driving the motor car in which she arrived, so she is of the servant class. And, so, an Imperial Officer to hold the door for a *servant woman!* . . . Well, that's America for you!

And then coming closer he suddenly saw with a shock that this General, with the gold epaulets and spectacular cap (but no medals, that was odd), was in fact his dear friend Sascha, Count Ivanov.

11

Old customers trotting into the hotel for lunch that day were greeted to the scene of their favourite Waldorf character, the Russian guy with the funny accent and the fake aristocratic manners, laughing and crying at the same time and embracing and kissing on both cheeks another Russian (only they were speaking French not Russian). And, for the moment, quite abandoning his duties as doorman of the Waldorf-Astoria Hotel.

Over the next few days Sascha was as good as his word, and brought his friend into the hotel business as promised. He also provided living quarters for Vasily that were at the same level of elegance as his own. Furthermore, it turned out that the night doorman at the Waldorf had reported for duty drunk, that very day, and was to be fired. Sascha Count Ivanov had always been considered a great catch by the Waldorf's management. The General announced that he had another royal, a friend who would consider — but only out of loyalty to his friend the General, of course — would consider filling in on the night shift until his, ahmm, yes, Trust Account and other funds could be liberated from those dreadful Bolsheviks and shipped from St. Petersburg. The managers were delighted. Vasily was fitted for a uniform equal in grandeur to the General's, and started work three days later.

But there was a sadness in his life, a big sense of loss. Two weeks later, as he sat in the shabby two-room cold water walk-up apartment he shared with his friend, and stared at the grey shape of his beloved Astur stamping angrily back and forth on her makeshift block, yearning to fly and to hunt, he knew that it was impossible to keep a goshawk in a tiny flat on the lower east side of Manhattan. And he also knew that he was going to have to return her to the wild, and that soon the last material vestige of his privileged life under the Holy Rule of His Sainted Majesty Nicholas, the Czar of all the Russias, would be gone.

He had tried to fly her in Central Park, but she had roused at a miniature schnauzer puppy, whose indignant mistress went looking for the police. A few minutes later as Vasily stood at the edge of Central Park Lake, by the Cherry Hill Landing, surrounded by a dozen children who gazed at the proud bird with a fascination that she found quite vulgar, two uniformed men came up to him.

"Citizen," said the older of the two, "what's the story about the falcon?"

"I am not being a citizen exactly," Vasily said cautiously. "Only a poor refugee from the evil Russian Revolution, isn't it? And she is not a falcon exactly, but a royal goshawk. Her name is Astur the Magnificent.

She is the only thing I was able to be bringing with me, from the St. Petersburg. But now I am afraid . . ." Here he had to stop and wipe a tear from his eye.

"Well, son, you can't bring her into the park, you know. We had a complaint she went after a poor little dog, see. That thing is too dangerous. She might even go after one of these here kids. So you better come with us."

An older gentleman in a frock coat, striped trousers and a top hat had been watching all this from the side. "Officer," he said. "I know a little bit about hunting birds, and I would like to talk to this man and suggest what he might be able to do. I have a carriage here, and I'll drive him out of the park. You have my word. And perhaps we can come to some arrangement."

The old gentleman spoke with a quiet authority. The policeman was impressed, touched his knuckle to the edge of his cap, and said, "Well, sir. I hope you can. Seems like a nice enough young fella. And the bird is very fine. But we can't have her doing what she does here in the park, you know."

"Of course," said the old gentleman. "Young man?" And he motioned Vasily courteously towards the fine black carriage just up the slope on the gravel road that winds through this part of the park, where a uniformed driver stood stroking the muzzles of a

fine pair of dappled greys who stood patiently between the shafts.

"My name is Olmsted, Charles Olmsted," he said,
and held out his hand. Prince Vasily shook it warmly.
"You are being so very kind. I am Vasily Prince Voyeikoff, of St. Petersburg. Although to be telling you
the truth, I am not sure it is being good to remind
American peoples that I am a prince any longer or
so."

Mr. Olmsted chuckled. "Climb aboard," he said.

They drove south towards the main entrance on
Central Park West. "My father Frederick Olmsted
designed this park," the man said. "Even before the
Civil War, when he was a young man and New York
was much smaller than it is today, he foresaw that
this great city might grow so fast that it would lose
sight of the trees and the grass and the water, and
that the people of New York would be much poorer
without those things. And wildlife too. So he designed a zoo for the park, you see. And built it right
after the Civil War. And I do not think—I am not sure
exactly, but I do not think that there is a goshawk in
the zoo. You could visit her every day. She would be
caged, of course, but in the open, with some room to
fly. And I am sure that the keepers would welcome
your instructions on her care and feeding. Henry?"
he said. The driver turned around. Mr. Olmsted

gestured in the direction of the zoo and the greys were swung to the left on a lane leading off to the east.

Vasily tried to imagine his proud huntress in a zoo, living with strangers. The carriage came up alongside the zoo and stopped. Behind the link fence two herons waded at the edge of a small artificial pond. Two cottontail rabbits nibbled at some lettuce leaves close by, and a plump brown speckled partridge led a quartet of fluffy chicks up the slope towards a set of hutches and a feeding tray. Vasily began to laugh.

"Excusing me very much," he said after a moment, and began to explain about the herons, the rabbits, and the partridge.

Half an hour later the ragamuffins and street vendors milling along the sidewalks of Houston Street East were astonished to see a most elegant carriage pull up outside the shabby old tenement building at number 321, with a uniformed driver and a distinguished gentleman in morning dress. He courteously shook hands with that funny proud Russian guy with the pet eagle who lived on the third floor with the General. The kids gaped and called out a few rude words, but a cop swinging a nightstick came rolling by and gave them a menacing nod of the head to shut them up, and then nodded deferentially to Mr. Olmsted. The old gentleman opened the door to the

Prince, who bowed deeply. He lifted his gloved fist, looked around, stepped to the street with dignity, and turned back towards the carriage.

"I shall have to be giving her her freedom, is that what you would agree, sir?"

"Well, we speak highly of freedom here in America, you know. But we don't all know how to live with it as well as we might. Will she be able to?"

The hawk, restless, made to rouse. She knew she was coming back to the dark shabby rooms upstairs, a hateful, undignified place. But there might be some of the fine beefsteak that Count Ivanov brought home from time to time. Ivanov was friendly with a woman who worked in the Waldorf kitchen. Astur was hungry, having missed her chance at the schnauzer.

Vasily bowed again, and went in.

The last excursion steamer up the Hudson, at the end of that season, left the 49th Street docks at 9 a.m. on the last Sunday in October. Vasily came home from work at midnight Saturday, got up at five, lifted the sleepy hawk into the parrot cage, put the hood on her head and the cover on the cage, and started walking across town before six. He was one of a very few passengers that morning. Most of the others had sandwiches in brown paper bags, for lunch. No children. Mostly old people. Vasily sat on a bench with his hand on the covered cage and watched the bustling city flow by, and then dissolve into pinewoods and open fields as they passed the north end of Manhattan Island.

As the steamer came abreast of the West Point Military Academy, shortly after 1 p.m, and began her circuit of the wider part of the river just north of the steep cliffs, to turn herself around for the run back downriver to Manhattan, the Prince stood at the after rail on the top deck with his hawk on his fist and removed her hood. She opened her wings immediately, in a half rouse at the clean forest smells and the glare from the river. Her head swung sharply from side to side.

"You may have some trouble with this freedom thing, my royal queen," Vasily said (in French, of course). "But I have faith that your instincts will be stronger than your education." She looked at him for a moment, but the keen air and the sunlight had given her a sense of eagerness she had not felt for months. She was scanning, not for prey exactly, but because she could not help scanning as soon as the hood came off. And perhaps she did not know it, but her instincts were looking for a forest. The tiny Pakistani bells on her jesses rang faintly in the breeze. "I will leave you the jesses. Perhaps they will remind you of me from time to time," said the young man.

He looked west towards the wooded hills north of West Point. He raised his gloved left arm a few inches. "You are my great love, and my first love," he whispered. "Be fierce, and be strong." He closed his eyes and swung, and felt the claws release and leave him. When he opened his eyes again Astur was circling high, to the west. The steamer had already begun its southward turn for the journey back. Vasily crossed to the other side of the deck and peered after her. Then he looked down over the side, took off the glove, threw it wide, and watched it circle like a dying bird down towards the waves. He picked up the cage and threw it too.

The hawk came back just once, over the steamer. She could see the familiar figure of a young man there, but there was no glove on his fist to come

"Be fierce, and be strong."

back to. To the west there were trees, thousands of trees. Their piney scent came to her on the west wind and something deep inside spoke to her. She turned away from the boat and the man.

He narrowed his eyes, leaned forward and peered until the dark shape was only a spot and then vanished. He reached into a pocket and pulled out the velvet hood, in royal purple, with the royal crest picked out in gold thread. He dropped it over the side and watched it sail off in the freshening wind. And that was that.

❧❀❧

A nd that had been two years ago, a considerable time in the life of a goshawk. Two years during which she had quickly been lured further and further north by winds and forest scents that reminded her of something deep within. She had at last found a combination of lakes and granite and pines that felt like home, and had rejoiced in the splendour of the game in that protected park where she could hunt but men could not. Over the last year she had begun to notice a little slowing of the responses, a little dulling of the edge. At first there was a run of near misses that made her cross and confused. For some weeks now there had been complete failures like this morning's. Each of them left her frustrated and famished. And now she was reduced to quitting the forest for the safe but not very satisfactory run of mice and voles and squirrels in the open land. It was demeaning to a royal personage.

Halfway to the hayfield, on the edge of the wilderness park's forest, but still inside the thick woods, Astur passed low over a stream that gurgled down into a quiet pool. And the water reminded her that, hungry though she was, she wanted a bath. Scouring the area for the presence of dangerous animals, particularly humans, she satisfied herself that she would be safe enough. Opening up the finger-like primary feathers at the end of her sails (the fourth feather is the longest in a goshawk), she glided softly down to the edge of the still pool. For a moment she stood still, listening carefully and looking around: a lady about to bathe needs her privacy. And then she stepped daintily into the water until it was up to her covert feathers. She crouched quickly and splashed a shower over her head with her sails. The water was icy. The stream had only recently lost its winter cover; there were still cakes of ice along the edges. She breathed deeply and repeated the shower, and shook herself dry as she stepped out. Then she looked over her breast feathers carefully and preened a few loose ones and some specks of dirt, and had another good shake. She scanned the sky and was about to take off, east for the hayfield. But then she saw, for the second time that April day, what might turn out to be dinner. Without having to fly out of the forest.

An old heron, migrating back into the wilderness park (a bit early for herons, Astur thought), was flapping his slow, distinctive rhythm just above the treetops to the north, and heading west, steadily deeper into the dense forest the hawk had been regretfully about to leave. A bit big for a goshawk to attack, but lots of meat there, worth a try.

She let him pass over a line of black spruce, and then, the moment he was out of sight, and thus blind to her blitzkrieg attack, she took off like a badminton bird off the racket, like a projectile out of a cannon barrel.

The heron never saw her coming. He was approaching a patch of open ground to which she would be able to carry the kill for a leisurely feast. She closed like a heat-seeking rocket grenade.

A goshawk in her few seconds of attack flight would be a terrifying sight if your eyes were fast enough to see what is for most of us a blur of accelerating feathers, talons and sharp-hooked beak. A beautiful sight, really, but the heron did not see it. Old and a bit dotty, dreaming of the nesting grounds not far away, and tired from a long day of ploughing along, *flap, slow flap, flap,* on what was meant to be the last day of his return from the south, he wasn't really paying attention.

Until, with the falcon's primaries humming like violin strings in her lightning-like strike, he heard rather than saw, rolled left at the last minute, flashed his own dangerous spike of a bill up at the blur of the plunging assassin, and lurched out of the way just in time.

Astur had to dodge that piercing upturned bill. So although she had her killer talons out and hooked and ready to foot the prey even before he was properly killed, she missed him. Plummeting past at that terrific velocity, before she could get her speed brakes out she was already in among the next line of treetops and floundering as she tried not to crash into them.

The heron shook his old head in amazement at his narrow escape. He began to beat the air with his broad, slow, concave wings, and rose at an impressive rate in a tight spiral, almost straight up. A hawk's bones are solid and very rigid; she's a hunter and her weapons have to be strong and sure. But a heron has fragile, hollow bones, to keep the weight of the big bird down. He is really light for his size, and those big parachutes sticking out of his shoulders can lift him up at an astounding rate.

The goshawk fumbled her way out of the spruce tops trailing some needles and a few bits of feather, perched on the first clear branch she could find, and contemplated the safe height of the still-rising heron. She had run out of the surprise factor. He would see her coming now, from below, too. Bad idea. She had no shelter, no stealth advantage, and he had that long sharp gimlet front end of his.

Astur began to mutter the rude French word a few times.

Then her penetrating eyes caught sight of something she liked to eat far more than herons. Herons, for all their fat bulk and plentiful muscle, taste pretty strong. They are frog eaters after all; and they have a taste that, well, they're filling but you remember it next morning when you're casting off the feathers and bones that collect as pellets in your pannell and you bring them up in the dawning light and spit them out.

But now, ambling slowly along the shore, right below her perch . . . O! O! There was a fat, delicious brown-ribbed, lazy, ruffed grouse. Who hadn't seen her. Well, she soon would.

Hawks like to "bind" or "truss" a grouse, their favourite delicacy, that is, to take it in the air and then bring it to the ground to devour.

Astur dived. As her speed built up she let out a long *Skreeeee!* to alarm the slow-moving ground bird. The grouse squawked and drummed, then looked up, screeched in terror as a kilogram of armoured feathercraft came hurtling down upon her at twice the speed of an express train, and she took off in panic.

The poor grouse had not even reached tree-top height and was still outside the safety of the thick woods, when a yellow razor-armed fist shot out and broke her neck in a single merciful stroke that sent her spirit off to fly among the mythic birds and the stars. Her heart was still pumping and the two birds were still locked together in the air as the falcon footed her hard, and ripped open the grouse's belly. Astur had already cleaned out and thrown away the intestines before they came to earth.

And in ten minutes there was nothing to be seen but a few wing and tail feathers, some drops of blood, and the entrails that had looped themselves over a branch where she discarded them on the way down, where the morning flies would get them, or a passing crow. Now there was a slightly sleepy, much happier bird of prey, cleaning her hooked bill with little clicking strokes of her claws and muttering small soft sounds of satisfaction deep in her soft, grey-white feathered throat.

It was late afternoon. Long shadows. Time to sail back to a safe roost in the deep woods and dream about the days of dignity and strips of fresh Ryazan filet mignon on a silver platter, and of a young prince who used to tease her breast feathers upwards with a small carved stick and tell her how very much he loved her.

For he did love her; there is no question about that. She was his first hawk, the first that was really his. His father Duke Ilya kept up to five or six hawks at a time, a couple of merlins, a shaheen from Persia, a taut, hard-eyed Greenland falcon, and one ancient and surprisingly gentle peregrine. And then, the day the young Prince turned ten, all the way from Vienna came this goshawk. At a huge price. (The gambling Duke had been lucky at cards that month.)

Astur was fledged, but still just a nestling; she had never flown in the wild. This kind of hawk is called an eyas, and she has to be taught to hunt. The letter of transfer said that she was known as *Astur Gentilis*. Duke Ilya was not much of a scholar, so he thought that was her given name, not the scientific Latin name of the species. (At that time. Now we say *Accipiter Gentilis*.)

"Come with me to the mews, *moy Knyazok*," said Vasily's father that fine summer morning in 1907. Russia was strong and happy in those days; at least it might have felt so if you were an aristocrat in St. Petersburg. War and revolution seemed far off, and the gambling Duke was not so deep into his financial troubles that he could not still talk to the money lenders, keep up appearances, and keep up his mews. He had taken a couple of weeks to make sure the new arrival was calmed down and sufficiently used to human company to accept the boy, who was going to be guided into manhood and princely responsibility by taking on the training of this quite clearly royal bird.

Some falconers prefer to train a passager, a wild bird who has already hunted on her own. Others like to envelop the infant bird with human presence right from the start, and that was what Ilya was doing with Astur, the eyas.

The Duke had actually slept on the floor close to her block, on the third, fourth, and fifth nights. He had waited a day until her hunger conquered her fear, then brought her warm, freshly killed rabbit on his thick falconer's glove when the first light came through the edges of the heavy shutters of the mews.

Of course the little ball of fluff was far too small and weak now to hurt the Prince's hand with its claws, but the gauntlet was part of the process; something she would become used to and come to trust as a place where food would appear.

"Come with me to the mews," Duke Ilya said to his son. "Because there is something there for you, and you alone. And the next and perhaps best part of your education is now to begin."

"What is it, Papa! What is it!" Vasily was hoping for a gun, a fine silver inlaid double-barrelled shotgun, perhaps, with his name worked into the engraving? "Not likely, though," he said to himself silently. "My father the Duke never hunts with a gun. Only with those birds of his."

But if "those birds of his" was a phrase that meant in any way that Vasily was not, well, in *love* with his father's hobby, the cold reserves he might have had began to melt in the spring sunshine when he saw the hawk.

"Now, Prince Vasily," said his father. "As well as learning to be a falconer—which is about the only practical and noble art still practised by the otherwise vain, useless, irrelevant and dissipated aristocracy you and I belong to—along with the falconry you will also be learning English. The English have all the best words for falconry."

But the Boy Prince was not listening. He was spell-bound. His new bird sat a bit nervously on its block and looked up at him with an eye that was not only curious and careful, but already held a hint of the pride and disdain for lesser beings that would become Astur's distinctive style, when she matured (and perhaps her downfall, or almost). Vasily reached out towards her, slowly, ever so careful not to alarm. The disdainful hawklet regarded him with suspicion.

Vasily had watched his father wooing other new hawks; he thought he knew what he should do. He quietly brought his left hand around behind the bird, and softly touched his gloved finger to the back of her legs, just above the feet. This is how you can easily invite a bird to step onto your fingers; from the back, not the front. At the light pressure from behind, the young goshawk quickly raised one foot and then the other, and stepped back onto the glove. Now, slowly, gently, Vasily brought up his other hand, the index finger crooked, until the knuckle touched her feathers at the breastbone. The little goshawk looked coolly down at the boy's finger. Vasily glucked softly in his throat, like the last drops of water going down a sluggish drain. The bird's posture seemed to relax a little. Vasily stroked softly upwards. Astur's eyelids drooped. She opened her beak.

Ilya the gambling Duke, who certainly did not want any injury to come to his handsome boy, was about to utter a word of warning about that small but already dangerous beak, but then thought better of it. Let him learn by experience.

The open beak descended towards the stroking finger. The boy paused. The beak surrounded the finger. It nibbled gently.

"Papa," said Vasily Ilyich Voyeikoff, third of that name, heir to a fast-disappearing fortune and a noble coat of arms, "Papa . . . I think I know what it means to fall in love."

"Papa...I think I know what it means to fall in love."

It was days and nights, and then weeks and then months. A young hawk taken from the nest in the wild, an eyas, has to be treated at first in a way that makes her feel part of the time as if she is still in the wild. This is not easy because it is not true; and hawks are good at telling the difference.

"Do you think you are patient enough to stay with this?" Vasily's father asked the boy one evening, as they shared a decanter of dark French wine. "If you are really going to train this bird yourself you might want, at the start, to spend a few nights with her in the mews, and be prepared to wake up and speak softly to her if you hear her moving on her block in the night."

Stay with it! Vasily could hardly wait to be on his own, in charge, out of sight of the aunts and the fussy servants. If he had had the word in his language then, he might have said that it was cool, real cool.

And so he began. He sat beside her when she settled down in the mews, no lamps or candles and the shutters closed tightly. At first light in the morning, he would bring his hand up behind her feet and press lightly against her ankles until the young hawk stepped backwards onto his gloved fist. Then he would loosen her jesses, which had tied her to her perch, and carry her quietly outdoors.

"The mews face east, you know," his father said. "So that the hawks can have the first light. They are very fond of the morning sun, and it is very beneficial to them. And when you bring her out every morning, as soon as the sun appears, she will come to think of you as the one that brings the sun to her. So she will come to love you."

Now Duke Ilya, the father, may have believed that it is true that a hawk can learn to love a human. But she is, after all, a wild creature. Whatever happened in the evolution of dogs and cats to make them so comfortably a companion of the hearth and the home never happened in the evolution of the hawks. And even cats and perhaps dogs, left alone in the woods with no person to feed and stroke and comfort them and talk to them, will become wild again, especially cats. Nowadays falconers don't talk about the birds learning to love the human; they talk about "imprinting" the hawk with the human presence. You can choose whichever word you like best.

In any case the young falconer must be with the bird constantly, so that her instinct to be wild and wary of all other creatures can become submerged under the comforting cloak of her reliance on the human's hand, the food he brings, and his voice.

Vasily had invented this "Gluck gluck" like the last drops of water going down a slow drain, and the throaty sound seemed to appeal to young Astur. If Vasily heard her rouse in the night, all he had to do to calm her was make the clogged drain sound softly, deep in his throat, and she would settle again. Or if she were especially restless he might go to her and stroke her mail, that is, her breast feathers; and she would gently nibble his finger in response.

Outdoors in the morning sun he would carry her for an hour, and then bring her a breakfast of the best Ryazan filet mignon, raw of course, followed by some bits of fresh-killed baby chick, including the wing with some feathers and bone in it, to make up the cleansing roughage that hawks need. The feathers and bone fragments form into a ball, the casting, in her second stomach, the pannel, which is like the gizzard in a chicken. Vasily learned to make sure the goshawk had brought up her casting before he brought breakfast. If she had not, he would carry her for a while, then put her on a perch, with her jesses, and wait till she cast before feeding her.

Then, once she was fed, he would climb to a raised platform at roof height, and leave her for a few hours on a perch higher than anything else around her, and stay in sight but down on the ground. Now, of course, if she saw something that made her feel like rousing and flying, she couldn't, because of the jesses. She would bate, which means she would fly up and tug, in vain, at the jesses. Then the falconer knows she is ready. So about noon Vasily would put a leash on the swivel where the jesses joined, and carry her out into a field and throw her up for a short flight, around him, on the leash.

In this way, she became restless to be flying free of the leas and the jesses, but at the same time comfortable and trusting with her boy falconer, and, most important, confident that he would bring her food.

Imagine doing something like this. Vasily was with his goshawk twenty-four hours a day. He did not play football or swim. His fencing master came to him for an hour every morning while Astur was on the high perch, and he practised his thrusts and parries where she could keep an eye on him. A servant set a table for his meals in the yard when the weather was good, or in the mews when it rained. He saw the Princess his mother, or his friends or anyone else, only if they came to visit at the mews or in the yard. He slept under a royal crest-embroidered quilt on a straw mattress on the straw floor of the mews, close by the goshawk's block. The bond between bird and boy grew stronger every day.

One day, while finishing his breakfast of smoked trout and coffee, Vasily saw his young friend Prince Alexei come jauntily into the yard. Alexei was carrying a shotgun. It was a brand new shotgun. It had engraved ornamentation on the sterling silver that encased its stock, with Alexei's name inscribed there too. It had two barrels that gleamed dangerously blue in the morning sun.

"I am going to get some rabbits," Alexei said. "Why don't you come along? I'll let you fire my gun, if you like. Look, I've got a whole bag of cartridges. They come from Germany."

Vasily hesitated and bit his lip.

"Oh come on, you goose. Your hawk'll be safe for a while. I heard what you're doing, and that's fine. But you were the best shot in our class at the Royal Youth Hunt Club, and I'll bet you'll be brilliant with this gun when I show you how to use it."

"You don't need to show *me* anything about guns!" Vasily said with a laugh. "All right then. Come on. Let's go." At the gate to the yard he said to the old servant who sat there to keep out strangers, "Look, old fellow, I'm going shooting with Prince Alexei for a while. You keep an eye on my goshawk, here's a copper coin for you. If she bates a lot bring her down and tell the kitchen to bring her steak, you've seen me give her steak, haven't you. Do you know what that means, 'Bate'?"

The old fellow looked at Vasily sadly. "Master Vasily," he said quietly, "I was Master of the Mews before your father was born. I ain't able fer it, now that I'm old. I been with your family sixty-one years, I have, and mostly with the mews and the stables. So I kin do what you ask. But I never seen a young falconer leave his charge when she's in hack like

35

this, not before she's had the hood. And I just don't think . . ."

"Your job is not to think, old man. I shall be back before she bates anyway, so just keep a close eye on her since you know so much," said Vasily, his hands itching to get at the shotgun. "And remember, I am *Prince* Vasily; not Master Vasily, if you please."

The old man touched hand to forelock and bowed, though his eyes were burning with disapproval. Vasily squinted up at the silhouette of his goshawk on the high perch. If Astur the Magnificent saw him looking at her she gave no sign. The two boys went cantering off towards the woods.

Some time went by. In fact it was high afternoon and the sun beating down severely when Duke Ilya came back from the city and sauntered around to the mews to see how things were going with the goshawk. He found the old gatekeeper fast asleep on his bench. There was a muted *screeee* from somewhere above him, the sound of feathers beating, jess-bells clanging.

The Duke frowned and tried to see what was happening on the high perch, but the sun was in his eyes, even after he moved around the yard. He climbed an exterior ladder leading to a loft, and the thirsty goshawk came into sight, pulling at her jesses and beating exhaustedly against their restraint.

The Duke muttered the rude French word and ran to the mews where he expected to find Prince Vasily dozing. It was dark inside. He flung open a window and the sun flooded in. Nobody. His face burned with anger as he headed, short of breath, towards the staging up to the high perch. Then he heard his son's voice calling, "Father! Father!"

Two small figures were struggling towards the gate, one limping badly, the other trying to carry him and drag him along at the same time. Prince Alexei's right leg was wrapped in torn strips of his elegant Spanish silk shirt, and the silk was saturated with fresh blood.

"He shot himself, Father! I knew I should never have gone off and left Astur, I knew it! But the gun was so beautiful, Oh please forgive me, you know how I've always admired a fine gun, and he was going to let me shoot it, that's what he said anyway, but when I asked him to let me try he just teased me and kept running ahead of me into the woods. Then I thought, you know, he was just, he never really meant to let me try the gun anyway, and I knew, it was so clear, Father, I knew I had to get back to my beautiful Astur. And I turned away. Prince Alexei was climbing over a fence. Can you imagine? He was carrying the gun loaded and the safety catch off. I heard the shot. I ran as fast as I could. I was afraid he would die!"

The Duke was relieved, angry and alarmed all at once. He glared at the old servant, now very much awake and blinking wide-eyed at the blood and the ashen-faced Prince Alexei stretched out, bent double with pain, on the sandy ground.

The Duke said, "Dzherenyoff, bring that goshawk down and water her and hood her. Half close the windows before you get the hood. She doesn't know you and she may be alarmed, but she is so exhausted . . ." The old family servant touched his forelock and began to climb.

"Father, let me do that," Vasily said, and pushed the old man aside. "Please look at Alexei's leg. I'll be right back."

For the next two weeks Vasily took his breakfast at his mother's table before slipping back out to the mews to sit by his goshawk. For the first few days the bird flinched and screeed whenever he approached her.

One morning he told himself to sit very still and try to make his mind enter the goshawk's mind, calmly and affectionately, with no other message than his loving presence. As he focussed on the small, stern head, motionless except for the occasional slow closing and opening again of the eyelids, the whole room seemed to become dark and silent, although sunlight was shafting down the dusty air from the half-opened windows, and the morning noises of sweeping and carts were clattering softly across the yard. His father's hand had been resting softly on his shoulder for several minutes before the young Prince felt it.

"It will be all right," the Duke said. "She is ready, I think, for some kind of gesture from you. I'll suggest something in a moment. But I need to talk about something else first."

"Yes, Father."

"About the gun. The gun that you wanted so badly that you followed Alexei away from your duty when he came to you waving one just like it. Perhaps one that was even better than the one you had dreamed of."

Vasily sat very still, feeling the cool steel of those barrels in his hand, although he had never touched them. He turned and looked up at his father's tired, thoughtful face.

"A gun is a beautiful thing, *moy moliny Knyazok*, my dear young prince. (He on occasion spoke a few words in Russian, just to show that he knew how.) It represents some of the finest craft and invention that we human beings have ever made. The gun has built great nations, and has led great adventures. The best of them are so beautifully made that it would be a very dull prince indeed who could resist their fascination.

"You see," the Duke went on, "while it is clear that you were wrong to abandon your charge, this beautiful living thing, because of your fascination with something that is designed only for death, all the same we do know that the great skill of this lovely creature is the skill of death, as well. And I want you to know that while I am sorry that you abandoned one agent of death for another—and we both know that you made a mistake . . ."

He was silent for a while. He saw that he did not need to further elaborate his message; so he waited for it to settle in the boy's mind.

"Now," he said. "Why have you not taken her up?"

"Father, I thought that if I stroked her mail, like that very first morning, then that would be the way to begin making friends again. But the moment I brought my hand near her breast she screeed and began to rouse."

"Well, she needs to touch you all the same. And I think you may have forgotten something. Suppose she were just to perch on your finger for an hour or so, with no movement except the faint pulsing of your blood beneath her claws?"

The boy remembered. Ever so slowly he moved his gloved left hand behind the crossbar of the perch. The goshawk did not move.

Slowly, even he could hardly detect his own movement, he moved his hand forward now until the extended fingers were nearly touching the crossbar, then slowly, slowly, upwards until they were behind the hawk's legs and just above her fierce, curved claws. He looked at his father; the father nodded softly. Vasily brought the hand forward so that the index finger in its thick, tough leather just touched those legs, then pressed, just a little. There was a pause, and then the bird, who really had no choice, stepped backwards, gripped the gloved finger with her scimitar claws, and rested.

Vasily did not even hear his father leave the mews.

Hawks and falcons are watchful birds. Their eyes are their most powerful sense, and they respond powerfully to everything they see. And so, when the falconer begins to train a gyrfalcon or a peregrine to be at ease with other people and strange places and dogs and horses, he carries her on his thickly gloved fist with a hood on her head. Once she gets used to being hooded, the first loose-fitted hood, called a rufter, will be exchanged for a personal, close-fitting hood that does not let in the slightest light.

Strangely, falcons seem to find the hood a comfort, not a restriction. And then, in the field, when the hunting lessons begin, when the hood is taken off she is instantly very alert to everything she sees, and quickly excited by the movement of any other animal.

"Vasily, my princeling, *moy malinky knyazok,* I am very proud of you," said his father, coming to his son in the mews one morning before the sun was up. "I have been watching closely, sometimes when you did not know I was nearby. And you have been steadfast, and the bird is ready for the field, and you can now go back to sleeping in your bed, and taking your meals with us at table. Here. I have brought you her lure. You will feed her from this from now on. You will swing it in a circle around your head, a wider circle each day, and then when she is used to coming to it for her beefsteak, we shall be able to let her fly free, because she will come after the lure whenever it appears."

"It looks like a tiny leather pillow, with feathers on the outside instead of the inside," Vasily said.

"Yes, and we'll tie her beefsteak to it here, with these old jesses, and a bit of chicken wing or head too, for her castings, and she'll get the idea that if she goes after a flying thing that has some feathers on it, she'll get something good to eat."

Ten thousand kilometres west of the Voyeikoff family mews, at a slightly lower latitude — and many years later — a fine goshawk, now growing older and a bit stiff in the joints, perches sleepily on the dead branch of a tall oak in a deep wood, digesting a much needed meal of fresh-killed grouse and dreaming of a park and a fine house, of slivers of beef on a silver spoon, and of the warmth and companionship of a boy.

"Vasily, my princeling, I am very proud of you"

Chapter Two

Wittgenstein

In another part of the forest, a newcomer to this wilderness park is having a much less satisfactory night. This bird is *quite* a lot smaller than Astur, but also quite a lot smarter. Small as he, is you would have no trouble seeing him, even in the dappled forest light. He is bigger than a sparrow but not as big as a robin, built quite a lot like a regular parrot in a cage, but smaller and much better mannered. And he is very colourful: yellows and greys, a red-orange slash under his beak, and a touch of brilliant blue on the head. Big eyes for a little bird. He is a seed-eater, not a predator.

All right, he's a budgie. A budgerigar, if you want his formal name. His proper name is, wait for this, Wittgenstein! Which would be hard to explain if you didn't know his story, so let's start with that. To say his name right, try "Vitgenshtine."

Wittgenstein had, until quite recently, lived with a man named Henry Harley, in an old log house on an unworked farm in the Mulmur Hills, not far from the sparkling waters of Georgian Bay. Henry Harley, in his day, had been a distinguished professor of languages at not only Harvard University, in Massachusetts, but also at Cardiff, in Wales, and the quiet little Mount Allison University in New Brunswick. But he had grown tired of the politics and bureaucracy of university life, and had taken his small pension to this log cabin in Ontario where people said he was retired.

He was not retired. He was going to write THE book that would, in the end, prove that the order of words that make up human languages was based on a mechanism deep inside the human brain, a mechanism shared by human beings all over the globe, whatever their race or culture. He knew a lot of languages. And he became fascinated when he found that he could teach languages to a bird, whom he thought much better company than all those stuffy old professors he used to have to work with.

And so Wittgenstein . . . (Henry Harley borrowed the name from an eccentric young philosophy student he had met in England) . . . Wittgenstein grew up learning to speak English, French and German, passable Italian and Spanish, a little Welsh from the Cardiff days, and a smattering of many other languages including Chinese and Swahili. In a sense,

Wittgenstein had everything. First, he was very good-looking. This is not to be undervalued. Good looks help to get every day off to a good start, though they can be confusing to their owner.

Second, the Professor made sure the colourful little bird had only the best things to eat, the kind of food that budgerigars would fight and die for, if they were free to fight and die for anything. He drank from a crystal siphon which was cleaned every morning and refilled twice a day with distilled water so that no nasty germs would invade his precious bloodstream. He had millet seeds and pumpkin seeds and guava from Australia. He had shredded coconut and crushed oyster shells and slivers of dried mango. He had a mirror to admire himself in and talk to himself in. Every morning a scratchy record player with a big horn on top of it was set to play softly by his cage, and although he did not know it, the music was by Bach and Scarlatti, which everyone knows to be very good for the spirit, probably even of birds as well as of people.

(But of course he was kept in a cage.)

The floor of the cage could be slid out, and was, without disturbing Wittgenstein, so that his messes could be cleaned up discreetly. The Professor would sometimes put aside his scholarly books and turn to publications on the care and feeding of budgerigars.

The publications came from Victoria, B.C. If there was anything a budgerigar needed (apart, of course, from flying freely around the house or anywhere else, messing wherever he felt like it and meeting and dealing with other birds), then Wittgenstein had it.

From time to time the Professor had a handsome visitor, a local lady who was, in fact, a famous newspaper reporter, who had decided to take some time away from the stress of daily journalism to think about life and perhaps write a book. She was even thinking of a book about the Professor, who had led a very interesting life indeed. And it is possible that the Professor, who was a bit lonely, was falling a little bit in love with the journalist. Her name was Kit, and she was good-looking, with a real spirit of inquiry flashing in her eyes, a ready laugh, a quick mind, and at just over thirty years of age a considerable reputation as a serious journalist. Henry Harley was eager to test his theories on her. Sometimes he lectured to her as though she were in a freshman class in linguistics at Harvard.

He would say, "You see, in China they say, '*Wo ai ni*.' And that means 'I love you.' Now in English, we cannot say 'You love I.' Because you can only love a 'me.' And the same in French. There is a bit of a puzzle about why the French put the 'love' at the end of the sentence, and the 'I' and the 'You' at the beginning. '*Je vous aime.*' You see. But the Chinese can just turn it around because they don't have an 'I' or a 'me', only a *Wo*. So if they say '*Ni ai wo,*' that means 'You love me,' you see. And we find in the very primitive languages that the *position* of the words, is, uhmm, is this all clear? And, and I am trying to demonstrate that the brain, well it is like mathematics and . . ."

But the Professor would get confused then, when he realized that she was smiling at him in a somewhat ironic way, and that must be because he had, well, he hadn't really meant to do all this talk about *love,* and perhaps she misunderstood him. Or perhaps she understood him very well indeed.

Henry Harley beat a retreat to his kitchen to cool off and calm down. He had a big old icebox in there. He chipped some ice from the big block in the top. Farmer Willis brought over a fresh fifty-pound block every few days. The Professor put the ice chips in two glasses and poured in some homemade lemonade.

While the Professor served her drinks, and small sandwiches that he made very precisely, the journalist would take Wittgenstein on her finger and say the same words to him over and over again. The words were "Freedom of speech is the first freedom."

Wittgenstein liked the sound of the words, though their meaning was a little obscure. The little bird knew a lot of words. But the meaning of words depends on your experience of the things that they stand for, and Wittgenstein had not got a lot of experience with freedom. The Professor had found a way to connect experiences with words, for the little bird. And they could talk about food, and about the mirror in his cage, and Henry Harley thought that soon they might find it possible to discuss ideas. But the subject of freedom had not come up.

Wittgenstein talked with the Professor all the time, but not with strangers. For a while the Professor had tried to get him to show off for the few visitors who came to the small house. But when Wittgenstein clearly was not willing to do that, the Professor came to think of their conversations together as special time, privileged time. As much as he was fascinated with Kit the journalist, he had not said anything to her about Wittgenstein's genuinely amazing ability to talk and understand. Not just English, but French and German, and a few words in those other languages as well. For now, he thought. Maybe later, when we know each other better. Now she wouldn't believe me, and I am not sure Wittgenstein would be willing to prove me right. So not a word.

Wittgenstein also never said a word to Kit, but he came to look forward to the journalist's visits, and always felt a little — well, *deprived* — when the journalist put him back in the cage in order to concentrate her attention on the notes she was making about the Professor's life and work and Great Ideas.

Then Wittgenstein would comfort himself by running the sounds of the journalist's warm, musical voice through his little head, and trying to reproduce the feeling of that voice, very different from his own croaking or his pretty good imitation of the Professor's baritone. Without realizing it, he began, in private, to actually make a sound that was like Kit's voice. And one day as he sat on her finger, before she took out her shorthand notebook and began one of her long interviews with the Professor, Kit, instead of trying to get Wittgenstein to talk about freedom, was busy listening to an unexpected declaration of, well, affection from the Professor. He had finally faced up to the fact that that she must know anyway, he had used that word so often in his little lectures.

Wittgenstein, unexpectedly, felt quite excited about the imagined sound of Kit's voice. And he walked stately as a parakeet up Kit's arm and onto her shoulder and nibbled at her ear, and said into it, in soft, precise tones, huskier than Kit's own but not far off, "Freedom of speech is the first freedom!"

The journalist leapt up as if she had been stung by a hornet.

"My God, Henry! Did you hear that! He said it, he said it!"

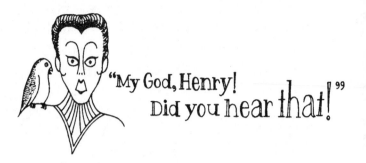

"My God, Henry! Did you hear that!"

Wittgenstein was alarmed by this shouting and wild waving of arms. He flew off erratically around the room crying, "Freedom of speech is the first freedom! Freedom of speech is the first freedom!" and when he got tired he lit in a high corner of the room on a ledge above a wardrobe.

He had never been up there before. It was very exciting to be so high and see so much. In what looked like a very big mirror on the far wall he could see trees waving their branches, all golden and scarlet with the fall colours. He started to fly towards that large glass, which had a strange fresh smell coming from it. But then Kit and the Professor began shouting at him to come down and the Professor waved an umbrella at him and he got confused and hid behind a tall lampshade and was not vigilant when Kit's hand came from behind, took him up gently and put him back in the cage.

But he had had a taste of something he had never tasted before, and a whiff of the air from that strange mirror-like place, a whiff that haunted him sorely, and he was restless and stamped up and down the perch in his cage with his heart pounding.

Now Kit was sorry that she had interrupted the Professor just when he was about to declare something about some very special feelings, and she led him into the kitchen and shut the door, because it was quiet and private in there. It is fair to say that both she and the Professor were confused by the emotions that were now out in the open. They were not noticing other things quite as clearly as they would normally have done. But Wittgenstein noticed everything. He noticed that the door of his cage, which Kit had latched carelessly, was not exactly the same as usual. He leaned against it, his heart thumping with excitement, and the cage door opened!

Wittgenstein stood on the threshold of *freedom*.

He stepped, a little uncertainly, onto the sill of that cage door, and looked around the room. Remember, every time he had been out of the cage before that he had been taken out on someone's finger. Of course he had been given a toss in the air, and had taken little exercise flights around the room, but always knowing that he was to return to the finger, and the reward of a little special food.

He looked up at that high corner he had just tried for the first time, and tried it again. He felt very different; different from anything he had ever known. From that high perch his eye was caught again by the big mirror-like thing where the tree branches were waving. He found that puzzling, and decided to investigate. Well, of course it was not a mirror at all. Wittgenstein tried to see himself in it, and couldn't, so he came closer and before he knew it he had stepped through it, and tumbled off the outer sill and threw out his wings, and began to fly. And. . . .!

He spent the first hour of his freedom flying higher than he had ever flown, over rolling hills he had never seen, over a world he had never imagined. The air was crisp with just a hint of frost. He had never felt cold air, and as long as he was moving he found it invigorating.

He forgot to be hungry; he even forgot to be as afraid as he had been for the first moment when he stumbled out of the open window, knowing perfectly well he was doing something he was not supposed to do.

He sprang upwards through the air like a skylark. He saw clouds for the first time in his life and tried to fly to one. It was too high. *"M'enfin!"* he said to himself, which is a phrase French people like to use when they haven't been able to quite do what they set out to do but want you to know that they have a good excuse. ("I mean, that cloud was really extraordinarily high, I *knew that*. I'll get the next one.") He thought the cloud might be nice to rest on. Like the pillow Henry Harley slept on at night.

Dizzy with excitement he flew off in all directions at once, taking no heed for the morrow. He laughed and chattered to himself in clichés from almost every language he knew. He lost sight of the house, he forgot the Professor, he forgot Kit. He was drunk on freedom.

He had never flown so much in his life and in a while he was tired, so he came down with a few chandelles and wingovers and inside loops and finally stopped, totally out of breath, on the top branch of a neighbouring maple tree.

A cat in the field below opened a sleepy eye and regarded the top of the maple tree sideways, as if it had no interest in the colourful little visitor who had just alighted there.

Presently there was a clatter and a flutter of air and another budgerigar sat on the branch beside him regarding him with a sarcastic yellow eye. This budgerigar was all black, with a coarse yellow beak and bad breath. Her feathers stuck out every which way and she had a permanent sneer.

"Where'dja get the nifty paint job, honey?" she inquired wittily, sucking on the mangled remains of a maple seed.

"Freedom of speech is the first freedom," Wittgenstein said, a little tentatively, not being used to conversing with strangers, especially one of his own size.

"Yeah, well, eternal vigilance is the price of liberty, kiddo, and if I were you I'd stop talking and start vigilatin!"

And with that, the other bird (for it was not a budgerigar after all, Wittgenstein realized; its feet were the wrong shape) clattered off noisily — on the wing — and Wittgenstein looked after it, blinking happily, but confusedly into the sunlight, unaware that a sleek, black, feline shape was now making its way silently up the tree trunk below him.

So unaware that he decided to preen. Preening is a vulnerable time, for birds or humans. They get focussed on themselves and their alertness to the rest of the world goes down. With each duck of the head into a wing or his breast feathers, Wittgenstein's view of his surroundings was eclipsed. The cat moved on each eclipse, up the rough-barked trunk, which gave him a good hold for his claws. To the first branch, then the second, then to the one about six feet below Wittgenstein, where he paused, only the tip of his tail, *flick, flick*, showing any movement. From a high branch in a nearby tree this was all being observed with some amusement by Wittgenstein's rough-talking new friend with the bad breath.

The other bird, who was a starling and thus very practical, found herself uncharacteristically inclined to interfere in the life-and-death drama that was unfolding beneath her. At the last moment she cackled down softly, "If you do not immediately start to flap them Day-Glo wings of yours, honey, you ain't gonna have no wings left to flap, and I don't mean maybe."

Wittgenstein was not used to hearing anyone speak like this, but there was something about the tone, rather than the content of the message, which caught whatever tiny portion of his brain was capable of taking things seriously. (When you are raised in a cage, on dried mango and the music of Scarlatti, and never have to make any plans, that part of your brain does not develop much.)

He shifted into "alert" and looked around just in time to see the cat's narrowed, golden eyes staring at him hungrily from a few wingspans away. The cat, surprised to be stared at, froze.

Bad move. For the cat. Wittgenstein darted a glance towards a spot just behind its left shoulder. The cat, wary and a little paranoid as hunters tend to be, followed the glance with a quick flick of its head. Second bad move. By the time he turned back to where his prey had been perched, Wittgenstein, panting with excitement, was sitting beside his new, feathered friend, on a twig too far and too slight to invite further feline foraging.

"You're new around here, aintcha, honey?" inquired the starling, with a sarcastic expression.

"Freedom of speech . . . " Wittgenstein began, but faltered, his heart still bombulating from the excitement of his near brush with Black Feline Destiny.

"I live in that house, over there," he said firmly (in bird talk, now, not human talk). He wanted to make sure the starling would know that the house made him important. "The one you can just see on the edge of the hill."

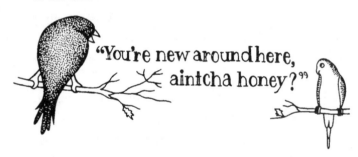

"You're new around here, aintcha honey?"

In the house on the hill, the one with the lace curtains, Wittgenstein's escape had been discovered. The sunny mood of the kitchen discussion about feelings and relationships had given way to the sounds of quarrel. The voice of the newspaperwoman had, for the moment, lost its softness and taken on a harsh edge of self-defence. Henry Harley's bald head poked through the window with the lace curtains under the October twilight and then he slammed the window shut, too late. The trees were in their autumn beauty, the woodland paths were dry, but there were no birds, of any kind, to be seen anywhere. No budgies, no robins, no eagles, no swans. Nothing.

Perhaps if Wittgenstein had sensed the distress his escape was causing, he might have flown to the window with the lace curtains and tapped on it with his beak, as he used to tap on the bars of his cage when he was hungry. Perhaps he might have been seen and readmitted with rejoicing and even a few tears. But then he would not have learned the extraordinary things he was on the threshold of learning. He would not have had the adventures that were now just around the corner, he would not have fallen in love, he would not have known the real meaning of liberty, and we would have had to stop the story right here, before it gets interesting.

So, on the whole, although the Professor and the journalist would probably not agree, it is a good thing that Wittgenstein did not go home that night.

In farmhouses around Mulmur township women were lighting coal oil lamps. Henry Harley was lighting candles. The room had calmed down. Outside, half a mile away in that tree, the air was cooler than Wittgenstein was used to. He found this bracing, but it made him hungry. His new friend, who had saved his life, but was a cool customer and seemed not to be offended by Wittgenstein's failure to acknowledge this, was not at all impressed by the house with the lace curtain windows. She was chewing another mangled maple seed. The sight of it made Wittgenstein's thick little tongue twitch. He knew that nobody was about to bring him any food, but he was too tired to do anything about it himself, nor did he have any idea where or how to look for something to eat. The last thing he sensed before falling asleep was that other birds were arriving in his tree and settling down quietly, as the darkness deepened.

Something woke him, perhaps the rasp of a clawed foot slipping on bark. In the moonlight he caught the reflection of a yellow eye with a wide, oval-shaped pupil, not three feet away, on an adjacent branch. As the cat sprang, the budgie pumped hard with his tiny legs and tired wings. He felt a tearing sensation as an outer primary feather was tugged from his flesh. He tumbled in the air, recovered before he hit the ground and, driven by his terror, fled upwards and away — anywhere away from that terrible beast — his shoulder aching and his flightpath a bit rough from the missing feather, the strange spectre of moon-shadowed trees terrifying him. He had never seen anything like it.

And when he ran out of breath and sank, exhausted, onto a telegraph pole by a railway line, he had no idea where he was. If he had stayed around to watch, he might have taken some satisfaction from seeing the cat tumble too, and miss the branches he screechingly reached out for, as twigs snapped at his falling body, until he landed with a *thump*—though on his four feet of course, as cats always do—clutching one bright yellow and grey but tasteless outer primary feather between his sharp front teeth.

November 4th, 1920
Professor Henry Harley
General Delivery
Creemore, Ontario, Canada

Dear Henry:

Sorry I had to leave so suddenly. When I got back to Mrs. Callaghan's in the village that night, there was a telegram from The Mail and Empire. I've been assigned to cover a major murder trial in New York. It is an opportunity I cannot turn down, as I am sure you understand. There was a late train that evening, and I just had to take it.

But I have to tell you that it is entirely my fault that Wittgenstein is lost. When we went into the kitchen the other afternoon I was really quite flustered by what you had said, and I know that I closed the cage carelessly, and that is why he got out.

You must miss him very much. I can only hope that with winter coming on he will come back to the one place he can count on to be warm and safe, and that he will be safe. I just thought how dangerous it must be for a tame bird in the wild.

But he is a clever little chap. And he will come back. And I hope you can forgive me.

Now in the meantime, I have been visiting the Waldorf-Astoria where some of the key witnesses in this trial are staying. I come on the streetcar from my little room on the upper West Side, and try to pick up some gossip and colour after the daily session in court closes down. I have gotten to know the doorman on the night shift, as he sees every-one come and go (it is an old reporter's trick, the hotel doorman). This one is _very_ good looking, and he is an amazing character. He claims to be a Russian prince who left because of the Revolution. But he speaks beautiful French. My French is not bad, as you know; and Vasily's English is terrible. So we speak in French and that seems to make him very happy.

But Henry, his French is quite extraordinary. He uses some expressions that <u>sound</u> French, but which I do not understand at all. And he will say things like "Ooh la, et Ooh la," instead of "Ooh la-la!", which is odd. And many other things which I am keeping notes on, because with your inquiry into the structure of all languages, who knows? There may be something here of benefit to your work, and then I will not feel so terrible about Wittgenstein.

Speaking of birds, this doorman claims that he brought one with him all the way from St. Petersburg, can you believe it? Is there such a thing as a Gozzuk? He tried to tell me the French name, but I could not understand it; it sounded like the word for author. He said this "Gozzuk" was the English word, but I suspect it may be Russian.

I am sure you are angry with me, for good reason. But I hope to see you again before too long, and that you will help me to continue with my article about your work.

Yours truly,

Kit.

PS. I am staying with
Mrs. G. Goodenough
149 E. 65th Street
New York City

The harsh sun woke Wittgenstein. His shoulder hurt. He looked inquisitively at the railroad tracks below, something he had never seen before. They had the kind of regular pattern that he had grown up with, like the patterns of books on shelves or boards in a floor. This reminded him of home, and home reminded him of food. He began to fly painfully along the tracks. Before long he saw houses ahead of him, a cluster of them, and the cool early morning breeze brought a delicious smell of roasting grain and seeds.

It was a village. In the centre of this little collection of sturdy wood-frame houses, with the odd prouder structure of soft yellow-grey or dark red brick, there was a low building with a shiny metal roof and a chimney that seemed to be the source of those aromas. Wittgenstein lit on a branch in a messy old box elder tree in the lane behind this little house and watched with interest as a boy lugged a heavy sack of flour out of a wagon and in through the back door. An old black horse stood between the shafts of the wagon with its nose in a feed bag. The boy came back out the door in a moment and threw a basketful of bread scraps and seeds to a group of pigeons who were walking about under the wagon, picking up oats that had fallen from the horse's feed bag.

The pigeons were bigger than the budgie, and looked very sure of themselves — not a feeling that Wittgenstein shared just then. They were chuckling and cooing in their thick grey throats, and greedily picking up seeds and bread crumbs. At first, when Wittgenstein flew down to the ground as near the pigeons as he dared, they paid no attention. He gingerly walked towards the edge of the group, picked up an oat seed, and crushed it hungrily in his beak.

It had a rough, country flavour, not quite what he was used to, but it went down very well, and in seconds he had pretty well forgotten the pigeons and was just scooping up seeds as fast as he could go, crushing them and swallowing them ravenously. He had just come upon his first scrap of bread crust and was cracking its crisp brown surface and enjoying the taste — unfamiliar in his mouth, but the smell of it was familiar — when he became aware that the world had gone very silent all around him. Just ahead of him on the ground, whence he was hungrily vacuuming up all this unfamiliar but satisfying food, there were firmly planted several sets of knobbly pink-and-grey pigeon feet. He looked up.

The pigeons had surrounded him. They were much taller and heavier than he. They glared at him with heavy, unfriendly eyes.

"*Currrdelley-oo?*" the Head Pigeon said, aggressively. Wittgenstein didn't understand their language but the meaning was clear, especially when all the other pigeons took a step or two towards him and the circle that enclosed him became smaller and even more uncomfortable.

"*Currrdelly-oo!*" the Head Pigeon said again.

"Excuse me," Wittgenstein said, and flew onto the wagon, where the black horse still stood patiently waiting for his driver. The pigeons glared up at him. On the floor of the wagon he saw more oat seeds, so he hopped down in there and gobbled a few. Two pigeons clattered up onto the driver's seat above him and glared and *currrdelly-ooed* again. When they moved closer to the edge of the seat he became afraid that they would pounce, so he moved to the other end of the wagon and kept on eating. The pigeons scolded again, and then consulted each other, heads together. Step by step, but silently this time, they moved quietly across the seat, down onto the edge of the sideboards, and step by step, their cross-looking heads nodding with each step, they came closer. Wittgenstein had taken enough harassment. He flicked up onto the roof of the little bakery and calmed down by speaking to himself quietly in two or three different languages, watching the pigeons feeding away below, evidently no longer interested in him whatsoever.

For what possible reason were these plump, grey, self-satisfied creatures getting all *currrdelly-ooed* over a small hungry stranger stopping by to share the baker's handouts? There was plenty for everyone. Wittgenstein found himself heartily disliking the pigeons. "They mess everywhere, right where they're eating," he said to himself. "And look at the stupid way they walk, with their heads bobbing up and down as if they had to check every step and see where they'd put their feet down.

"Which they probably do," he added out loud. "They certainly look that stupid."

"That's right, honey, they certainly does, and they certainly is," said a familiar voice from a branch in that box elder. "Butcha don't wanna mess with 'em. It's not they ever really gonna do anything to ya, it's all talk. But they feathers fulla horrible bugs and ticks and dust and stuff. I know I ain't too tidy myself, feathers kinda stickin' out here and there, But hey! I take a bath every chance I get. Not them. Not healthy, them pigeons. You don't wanna get close to them. You just hang out somewhere else till they move off. There's lotsa times in the day they never here. I come here every day, over from the bush where I metcha yesterday. Can't take too much of that crusty stuff they throw out here, but it makes a change from the maple seeds. Knowaddimean? You go home lass night? To the lace curtains? Whatcha doin here?"

Wittgenstein found himself unexpectedly pleased to hear a familiar voice, even if it was the starling with the bad breath. She had, after all, saved his life. She was his first friend since coming to the free world. And while freedom was exciting, if it meant being on your own all the time, things could get lonely. "Thanks," he said. "It's good to see you," and he joined her on the branch of the box elder.

"I didn't go home," he said. "I thought of it a lot when I got hungry. But I like it out here. I like the flying, and being able to go where you like and do what you want. But you pay a price. That terrible cat? And even those pigeons. *You* say they wouldn't have done anything, but they had me surrounded, you know. Anyway. You really have to watch out, don't you?"

"Yeah, well I noticed you was not too swift in that department," said the starling.

Wittgenstein followed her around the village for the rest of the day. She showed him a cornfield on the edge of town where the harvest had left the ground strewn with shredded leaves and stalks. If you were lucky there would be, here and there, a bit of a corncob that had broken off. The hard yellow seeds were almost enough to break your beak, getting them off the cob, but they were full of flavour. In a garden behind the Methodist church there was an ornamental tree with small, dark berries gleaming a rich red. They were sour, but easier to chew than the corn. Seeds were everywhere. Tiny goldenrod seeds on tall rangy plants along the roadside, and Queen Anne's Lace in curled up baskets that had once been delicate white filigreed flowers, very bitter; you wouldn't want them unless there was nothing else to be had. Same with the few milkweed seeds left clinging to burst pods on the tough, sage-coloured stalks: easy to chew but terribly bitter. The corn was best. On the ground in the woods north of town there were dozens of different colours and kinds of berries, even a few faded and dried raspberries that were delicious — you could eat the whole berry — and pulpy dark blue things growing close to the ground that had no taste at all, but were very filling.

And so for the next few days Wittgenstein and his gabby friend ate well. She enjoyed showing off her foraging skills and, for the most part, he enjoyed the food, and of course the company of this rough-talking, self-reliant, bad-breathed, bad-mannered, awkward-looking creature. But she hung out with him only for a few hours every day. Most of the time she went back to her gang, which seemed to be getting bigger. Once, he considered going with her, but he knew that while he could stand her chatter, to be with that non-stop crew would be too much.

As the days went by, clearer perceptions replaced his earlier romantic feelings about her (the first friend, you know, and remember, she had saved his life). She insulted him quite a lot. "Yer too dainty, honey. Y'll never get one a them seeds open if you don't just step on it and mangle the bajammers outa the thing. Sure kin tell 'at *you* grew up in a soft spot. Sure kin tell 'at you never went hungry." For a while he had found this kind of thing entertaining, but it began to get tiresome. And she did talk *all* the time.

The days grew shorter and the nights colder. Crowds of equally gabby, bad-breathed, bad-mannered, rackety-feathered birds of her own kind drifted into town and gathered by the hundreds on the single telegraph wire that ran along the railway. Wittgenstein's friend and advisor seemed to forget about him much of the time and go off more and more to gossip with these sometimes black, sometimes speckled, always rough-looking members of her own tribe. He didn't mind all that much. He began to explore a little more widely, and to try out seeds that his sharp sense of smell helped him discover, seeds that the starling had not even noticed.

At night, remembering cats and pigeons, he went high, and went deep. In the village he found a bit of broken brickwork just under the eaves of the Methodist church (where the ornamental cherry tree was). There were seldom any people in the church at night, and the broken brickwork made a kind of little cave, just big enough for him. Even better, there was a crack going right through to the inside of the building, and a small warm current of air came out through that crack and made his little cave quite cozy. The warm air carried a whiff of soap and tobacco and other human aromas that made him feel a bit wistful. But he was safe there in his little town house, and comfortable.

He found a country house, too. In the woods at the edge of town there was a ragged old basswood with many holes in a dead part of its messy jumble of trunks, holes that other birds must have been nesting in last spring. These holes were not clean, but there were layers of feathers in them, and some of them had comfortable nests of woven grasses and twigs and bits of string. He tried a few of these out as well, so that he had different places to go to almost every night, safe, and reasonably sheltered from the night air that grew colder day by day.

Every afternoon now those hundreds of starlings gathered on the telegraph line and chattered non-stop, yelled at each other, in fact, so that you could scarcely make out a word. He was sure they were not really listening to each other. There was a lot of scolding. "Yeah, well, you always talk like that and your stupid speckled kid is even worse," he heard once. But mostly it was just *yammer yammer yammer*. Until they would all lift off at once like raindrops parading off a wet branch when you smack it with your hand, down first and then up and then forming into a cloud of birds, you couldn't believe they weren't running into each other. And the cloud blowing off in this direction, then in that, settling down in trees or on a ledge under the eaves of the courthouse, where the chatter would start up again, *yammer yammer yammer*.

People called out to him, from time to time, when he was in the village, and that upset him a little. "Hey, look at that! Isn't that one of those fancy birds they have in pet shops in the city?" "No, I think it's some kind of a wild parrot or something." "Don't be silly, we don't have parrots in this part of the world.

Are you sure it's not some kind of, what do you call them, a grosbeak?" "No, I think it's some kind of canary that got away." "Canaries don't have any blue on them. He's too big for a canary."

Wittgenstein enjoyed hearing some human speech, but he felt uneasy all the same, suspicious of these people. They were a bit like pigeons, somehow. On the whole he kept away from them. One afternoon when it was quiet behind the bakery and the pigeons had gone off out of town, he drifted down among the yellow and brown leaves that were tumbling along the lane and lifting from time to time in the breeze. Some tiny white leaf-like specks were blowing among them, nothing he had seen before. When he picked one up in his beak it was very cold, and then it changed into water and he could drink it. It was a nice drink. He had a few more. And then, as he was picking at the bread crumbs the pigeons had left behind, the starling appeared.

"Well, hey pal, we're leaving. It's been grand to know ya. Watch out for cats. Mebbe see ya next year."

"Where are you going?" the budgie asked.

"Well, you seen 'em all on the wire? Do that every year, it gets cold like this. All go together. Head for the sun. Find some place where there's green grass and seeds and stuff still growin'. That white stuff you were picking up and drinkin' just now, I saw ya, that stuff, there gets to be too much of it, see, know-waddImean? So we're outta here, prolly this afternoon. Wanna come with us?"

"Well, no. Good luck, though," Wittgenstein said. And off she went. Well. So now he had nobody to talk to. But he was free to do whatever he wanted to do, and perhaps it was time for a change of territory, find something new. Maybe there would be a new friend.

The light snowfall ended and the sun came out. The budgie decided he was ready for a serious bit of flying, and headed out of town, turned right instead of left, and without realizing it was heading more or less in the direction from which he had first arrived, some weeks earlier. He soon left the railway and headed up into the nearby hills. Within minutes he discovered that instead of the new ground he had intended to explore, he was coming into familiar territory. Then, sure enough, there just ahead of him on the side of the hill was the maple tree where the cat nearly got him the first time, where he had met his friend, the loud-mouthed starling, and just beyond it the little house with the lace curtains.

Wittgenstein put on the brakes and stopped on a branch in the maple tree, now almost bare of leaves. With a pang of homesickness he saw the shape of an old man moving across the window, the same window he had stepped through into freedom, not that long ago. He felt a very strong need to talk to some-body who spoke nicely and didn't scold him just be-cause he had never been poor and hungry. He flew to the roof of the house and perched on the chimney where he could smell the familiar smells. He remem-bered the shredded coconut and the slivers of dried mango and felt that it would be very fine to taste those lovely things again. Then a funny thing hap-pened. As soon as he began to imagine the taste of them, he remembered the inside of the cage and the door that was usually locked. *That* part he did not like. Yes, the fancy seeds from Mexico and the dried fruit and the crushed oyster shells and the mirror, they were all very fine. But after a few weeks of free-dom the sensation — even the *imagined* sensation — of being caged again made him fidget. He flew around the house for a minute or two, thinking about this. Professor Harley stopped by the window, and peered out, and looked startled as though he had seen something, and began to undo the window catches in order to open it. Then Wittgenstein decided it was time to disappear, and headed back towards the railway tracks.

The few wisps of early snow had vanished in the sunlight, and the air was still mild as it began to get dark. Wittgenstein managed to slip in among the pigeons behind the bakery just long enough to get a few mouthfuls before they began that mindless *cur-rrdelley-oo* stuff at him. He decided that it was such a nice evening he would head out to the basswood tree and sleep there instead of in the cave under the eaves of the church.

He had flown into one of the abandoned nests, and was settling down as the darkness deepened, when he heard a deep, slightly gruff voice just outside his entrance hole, saying, "Excuse me." He hopped to the edge of the hole and looked out. A horned owl was perched on a branch close by, just another hunched dark shape among the crooked branches of the old basswood, so it was not entirely surprising that the budgie had not seen him when he arrived at the tree in the dark.

"I am bound to tell you that you are trespassing," said the owl. "However, as the former residents have apparently withdrawn for the winter, and as I believe your intentions are only temporary, I shall not notify the constable."

"The constable?" said Wittgenstein.

"As the circuit judge in these parts I am normally obliged by my oath of office to notify the raven, who is our constable on this part of the circuit, of any infractions or tenancy irregularities that come to my attention. Mostly real estate, I am sorry to say. Not many good, juicy crimes of vengeance or embezzlement even. Mostly just infractions. And the law says I have to notify, you understand. So I do that. But it is really not important at this time of the year when the migratories have all left.

"Still," he added, "I seem to have the habit, you know. Of telling birds when they are trespassing. Perhaps it is because there is so little to do in the winter, when my courts are not in session. I miss it. I rather enjoy laying down the law, I have to admit. Even when it doesn't really matter a hoot. Heh, heh. 'Hoot.' I hope you get the joke."

The owl bent his head over sideways to take a closer look at the little bird. Now Wittgenstein could see that the feathers that made up the horns above his ears were quite white, and much of the top of his head was white too. That gave him a look of age and wisdom. As he thrust his head even closer, those large yellow eyes reflected a glint of starlight. Now, even though much of the owl's body was just a large, vague shape, the eyes were startling. Wittgenstein took a nervous step backwards.

"No, no, step out here and let me look at you," said the big owl. "I don't believe I have ever seen anyone in quite as fancy a dress as that before. Unless, perhaps, you might count the orioles. They go a bit far, don't you think? There, that's better, let me have a look."

Despite the pompousness of the big bird, there was a kind tone to its voice that reassured Wittgenstein.

The owl said, "Well, I can certainly tell that you don't come from around here. And I sense that you don't feel at home, too. I may be a fat old judge who has sat on too many real estate cases and doesn't see enough of the raw animal drama of life and death issues, but I do have a sense of how birds feel about things. That is why I am very good at my profession, you see. And my sense is that you do not feel exactly as though you belong here, that you miss wherever it is you came from."

Wittgenstein said, "Where I came from I was kept in a cage. I was hatched in a cage and raised in a cage and fed and watered and talked to and instructed and pampered and admired. I didn't know what it meant to be free until they left my door open a few days ago and I discovered this wonderful world out here. Of course, it is a bit frightening sometimes. I think *you* are a bit frightening, although you speak very kindly."

He stopped to think for a moment.

"And of course, there is not very much company. I do miss talking. Talking to myself is not the same."

"No, it's not," the owl said. "But you can have talk and freedom at the same time, you know. I have to live on my own much of the time. We owls find that we generally manage our lives best that way. But my fellow judges and I meet together by a pond in an oak forest beyond the big lake, oh, every few weeks or so. And we talk for two or three days at a time, and we are very good companions. These other judges are not all owls, by any means. It is a secret society, and we are not allowed to name our members. But we do discuss the more interesting things, from all parts of the animal community, you know, and share our knowledge. And so we learn from each other, and hear about strange cases and wise judgments, you see? And then it is time to go back to the daily life of solitude. But we always know that we shall be getting back together again. Now, you look to me like an intelligent fellow, even though your outfit is a bit cheap. And I would think you could work something out so that you could have your fine food and your pampering and the good talk . . . and your freedom at the same time. That is what you look like to me, in any case."

Wittgenstein said, "I don't know how you can tell what I look like, it's so dark out."

"Ah," said the owl. "That's my specialty, you know. Seeing. That's why these fine yellow eyes of mine are so big. So that I can hunt at night. For my dinner."

"Dinner!" said the little bird. "Hunt?" And he stepped quickly back inside the nest, well out of reach.

"Ah," said the owl again. "Not for the likes of you, my boy. Moles and mice, those are my dinner these days, the odd small rabbit once in a while. But in this bit of woods—uhmm—the moles that run on the surface at night are my simple prey and my heart's delight. I hope you caught the rhyme there. Surface at night? Heart's delight? And the metre? I am rather good at rhymes. And at hunting. I just swoop down on them silently and carry them up here and enjoy my meal on the branch. And make up a rhyme or two. Or a joke."

The big owl gave a courteous nod in the direction of the nest, spread his broad, one-and-a-half metre long wings, and sailed off noiselessly into the dark. "All the same," Wittgenstein thought, "I think I had better sleep in my cave at the church from now on."

There was a small park in front of the church, with three oak benches in it and a little fountain. The fountain had a marble plaque on it that once said:

TO THE MEMORY OF

LIEUTENANT PETER OLIPHANT

AND PVT JAMES TREMILLS

THEIR NAMES WILL NEVER BE FORGOTTEN

Unfortunately, the marble chosen for this plaque was a kind that does not weather well, and already the two names were worn away and impossible to read. The fountain did not run in the winter, although there was usually a little water left in the basin, where Wittgenstein could get a drink. One morning the budgie awoke to find the ground quite covered with a layer of thick snow. He shivered as he stepped out of the warmth of his cave onto the edge of the broken brick to survey the world and think about where he might find breakfast. There were still some of those ornamental cherries, a bit dried and shrivelled but still tasty and satisfying, on the tree behind the church, and he thought he would start his day's feeding there.

Looking down at the park he saw the familiar figure of an old man striding energetically along the road, with an empty string shopping bag swinging from one hand. It was the Professor. Henry Harley paused to read the inscription on the fountain, wiped his glasses with a handkerchief, bent over and swept snow from the bench, and sat down to read more carefully and perhaps to catch his breath, as he had really been walking quite strenuously, for exercise.

"Hmmph!" he grunted. "It says their names won't be forgotten, but you can't read 'em at all. The marble plaque has forgotten, it seems."

When Wittgenstein heard the faint rumble of that familiar voice, he could not resist.

As the elderly scholar frowned, trying to make out the rest of the badly eroded inscription, something about the Boer War, it seemed, there was a flutter of small wings and a shadow flitted over his face. When he lifted his eyes from the inscription, there, sitting on the spout of the fountain with its dribble of ice, was a dear and familiar feathered creature. The two friends stared at each other silently for a moment. A tear came to the Professor's left eye, and then to his right. He tried to wipe the tears with the net bag but that didn't work, and he fumbled unsuccessfully under his thick coat for a handkerchief.

After a while he said, "But why, Wittgenstein? Why?" (Actually, what he said was, "*Mais pourquoi, mon Wittgenstein? Pourquoi?*")

The intelligent little bird thought for a moment. Perhaps there was an opportunity here. He leaned forward and stared the Professor hard in the eye.

"*Je n'aime pas les cages!*" is what he said firmly.

The Professor was quite taken aback.

"You don't like cages?" he spluttered. "You don't like *your* lovely cage, with its mirror and its crushed oyster shells? And those expensive seeds I get for you, sent all the way from Mexico? But, but what is wrong with it! It's the finest cage I could find. I keep it as clean as can be. It is sitting there waiting for you. What could possibly be wrong with it!"

Birds can't smile. But Wittgenstein felt something like a smile inside his tiny elegant brain. And he said, "Freedom of speech is the first freedom."

The Professor blinked in complete confusion now. The annoying little fellow was quoting his friend Kit, the journalist, whom he also missed — what in the world was she doing off in New York at a murder trial of all things? But then the budgie continued.

"Freedom of speech is the first freedom," he said again, "but the freedom to come and go as you please is the best freedom."

Henry Harley just sat there on the cold park bench shaking his head in astonishment. How could he have been so stupid? Here he had spent all that time teaching the bird to say words in several different languages, and even more wonderful, to actually be able to engage in a small amount of simple conversation . . . and it had never occurred to his old academic brain that this extraordinarily intelligent little, well, little *person* almost, might ever come to feel that being confined by metal bars was not the most agreeable way to live.

They walked together through the town, chatting. Wittgenstein rode on Professor Harley's shoulder. When they came to the General Store, Mrs. Spencer stared at the colourful little hitchhiker and said, "Well I'll be, Professor! Is that thing belong to you?"

Henry Harley was going to say yes, when he thought better of it and said instead, "Well, ah, he is a very good friend, who used to live at my house, and may indeed do so again.

"One day," he added. "Perhaps soon. We are discussing an arrangement."

"Well, I'll be," she said again. "Mitchell and me, we seen him peckin' at crusts out behind the bakery one day. Mitchell said he was some kinda canary. I know he wasn't no canary but that's what Mitchell said. So what kind of a critter is he anyway?"

"Well," said Henry Harley, "he is a budgerigar, or budgie for short. But I call him Wittgenstein."

And there was something about the way the Professor said his name, with such affection and perhaps with a new understanding, that led the budgie to feel that everything was going to be all right, after all. He would be partly right, and partly wrong.

For one thing, it was really good to be warm all the time. And the first thing the Professor did when they got back to the house with the lace curtains was to find a pair of pliers in his cluttered little tool box and use it to take the door off the cage. Wittgenstein stepped into the cage and admired himself in the mirror, and preened a bit, stepped onto the ledge again, and flew to that high corner above the wardrobe from where he had first become aware of the outside world through the big window. The Professor prepared a meal of the budgie's favourite things. The bird ate it with relish and chuckled and gurgled in his throat, and talked a wild crazy mix of bird talk and human talk, looking at himself in the mirror. He looked just the same, a bit dirty perhaps, but he could preen the dirt away. He looked rather fine, in fact. He fell asleep, awoke with a start to find himself in the cage again, then remembered the door, stepped out, flew to where the old Professor was snoozing happily in a big stuffed armchair, walked up the sleeping man's arm, nibbled softly on his ear, and said, "*Ça va très bien, n'est-ce pas?*" And for the next few months, that was so; things did go very well, didn't they?

Whenever the sun was out and the temperature not too low, Wittgenstein would hop to the window and tap on the glass with his beak, and then wait there until the Professor noticed and came to open the window. Wittgenstein would step outside, onto the sill, chuckle a friendly bird sound in his throat, as a way of saying, "I'm in the bird world now, but I'll be back later." And then off he would go, winging over the snowy fields, checking in at the edge of the forest to see if there were anyone there he might talk to. On nice sunny days he followed the railway tracks to town, and flashed down among the pigeons for a few seconds, more to annoy them than to eat, since he was eating perfectly well at home. He would visit his cave under the eaves of the Methodist church, peck at a few cherries in the tree out behind the church, and once or twice, just for fun, cruise out to the woods at the edge of town—to see if the judge might be around—and look in on the staggered pillars and hollowed-out nests of his ragged old basswood. He knew the way now.

Those were only on special days. More often than not, his daily outing would be composed of some flying exercises with rest periods on the chimney top, a few minutes right up on top of that maple where he had first met the starling, and then home again. But when he did make those occasional excursions to town, he would be away for the better part of the day, returning only as the sun dropped low in the western sky. On those days the Professor would begin to worry when he awoke from his afternoon nap. He would sit by the window and wait with increasing annoyance until the budgie turned up and pecked on the glass to be let in.

But he never scolded. And so they got on very well indeed. Wittgenstein had his freedom to roam *and* his warm bed, his mirror and his fancy food, and Henry Harley had his friend.

Now the days began to get longer again, and before long the welcome dripping sound of snow melting off the roof would be heard before lunchtime, and even a few bits of brown grass began to poke through the white on the south side of the ridge. There were new smells in the air when Wittgenstein went out for his afternoon exercise. One afternoon as he sat on the highest possible twig of the maple tree, he heard the faint sound of a great many voices calling out in wildly eager tones from a long way off. They seemed to be approaching, and Wittgenstein sensed that something important was coming his way. He took off and climbed high, so that the maple tree was just a smudge below him, and the house was so far down he could not make out the lace curtains. He circled slowly up there, looking off in the direction of the sounds.

At first it seemed like a blur or a moving streak in the sky, getting thicker and wider as it came towards him, a long ragged line stretching from east to west, and curving up and down like a wave as it grew, and approached, and began to resolve into separate shapes, bird shapes, big birds, ploughing steadily, *beat, beat, beat*, northward towards Wittgenstein's patrol zone.

"Honk honk! Crang crang!" they went, all muddled together, nobody listening to anybody else, all of them calling out joyfully and eagerly as they beat that unstoppable roadway in the sky, straight towards the North Pole. As they came beneath him Wittgenstein saw that they were strung out in several huge, flat Vee-shaped formations. Four or five Vees at least, with a leader at the point of each Vee who seemed to be doing less of the talking than the others, concentrating on the course, and every other bird obediently going up or down, or left or right, whenever the leaders altered course in the slightest.

Wittgenstein was well above them, so even though they were cruising north at a speed that was double what he could maintain, by diving down upon this glorious, magnificent crowd, pumping as hard as his little wings would go, he was able for a moment to keep up with them, just above and to the side of the lead Vee.

"Who are you? Where did you come from? Where are you going?" he called out.

"Wah-wah-wah-wah-water!" cried a female near the lead. "We have to save the water!"

"We are the soldiers of the springs and the redeemers of the rivers!" called another, a gander this

88

time, "The lords of the lakes. If we do not get to the lakes the sun will steal them and suck them all up into the sky. It is our mission. We go to keep water in the world. It is a mission. We are calling out to the lakes and the rivers that we are coming, so they will not lose hope. *Wah-wah-wah-wah-water. Honk honk! Crang crang!*"

Wittgenstein was unable to keep up with them after that. He called out, as the vast aerial parade began to leave him in its wake, "But the lakes have always been there, they've been covered in ice all winter, but they are always there."

"I've never seen a real lake," said a young gander, as he went by, "only the tiny pond in a city where people came and put water in it every day and fed us. But the elders have all told us that the real lakes dry up if we Geese do not come to save them."

The friendly youngster had allowed himself to fall behind in order to tell this to Wittgenstein, and the elders were *cranging* and *wah-wahing* and *honking* at him to join ranks, not be so sloppy.

"They tell us that" he called happily, as he pushed harder and got back into place, "So of course it must be true. Good-bye-*ah-wah-wah-wah.*"

"What a spectacular, glorious crew," Wittgenstein said to the Professor, when the window was opened to his tapping a half-hour later and he gave his daily report. He had watched them until they were out of sight, the lowering sun glinting off their brilliant wings that beat forever until they disappeared. "Is that right? What they said about the lakes?"

The Professor smiled a slow smile. He too had heard the great clamour of spring-announcing voices, and his heart had been lifted by the sound. So he said, "Perhaps. Perhaps, in some mysterious way. Perhaps it is true, after all."

Many times over the next few days Wittgenstein heard the same exhilarating clamour, but always from far off. He saw no more geese, but their hopeful, distant, mission-driven voices gave him a strange excitement too, a kind of wishing for something grand and significant. He did not know what. One day as he sat in a lower branch of the maple tree, listening to a far, faint hint of those voices, so faint he wasn't really sure, and at the same time rubbing the side of his bill against some swelling, reddening knobs on the maple twig, that had not been there a few days before, and were giving off a lovely light perfume, he heard a soft flutter of wings descending. He looked across to the other side of the maple, where a colourful creature — scarcely bigger than he — was settling onto a branch.

He thought her the loveliest creature he had ever seen, with the possible exception of his own image in the mirror on a particularly good day. She was green and golden, she was radiant and fresh; her feathers were a rich, subtle greyish yellow, blending almost into green partway down the primaries, which then became an elegant, pointed black. She made the sky gather again. It was all shining, it was Adam and Maiden. She looked at him with her head cocked slightly to one side for a moment, and then she opened her beak and said, "Hello-o-o" in a throaty, musical voice that made him tingle in a way that he could not remember tingling before. Wittgenstein gulped.

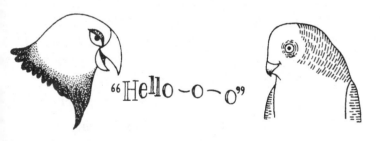

"I don't think I have seen you here before," he said.

"No-o-o," said the evening grosbeak. "I don't think you have. Nor I you. Nor have I ever seen anyone quite so, well, it may sound bold, so forgive me, but you are very, very handsome."

"Well, that's right," said Wittgenstein, having been told variations of the same thing all his life, and nobody ever having instructed him about not appearing vain or stuck up. In fact, he was not stuck up, just friendly and quite justifiably proud of his splendid plumage. "That's right, I am. And so are you. I don't think I have ever seen any bird in the wild who looks quite so fine as you; so we are a good match."

At hearing this, the other bird closed her eyes for half a second. Wittgenstein said, "And of course, I have never seen you around here before, either. Where did you come from?"

"Well," she sighed, blinking open again," my people held a going-away party last night, in upstate Ohio. We meet there every year outside an abandoned salt mill where there is still, well, a real treasure trove of salt in the ground. So, of course, it is a great party place. Do you love salt too? I expect you do. Anyway, I overdid it. On the salt. I keep saying to myself, 'Sweetheart, you really should go easy on that stuff.' But I suppose I never will. I still have a headache. And I guess I was still sleeping when they set out this morning early. So, they are probably already way off ahead of me. They might even have chosen the alternate year migration path. I can never remember those things. I always count on the boys for that, you know. Oh dear. Well, I don't mind now.

I just stopped in here for a rest and a drink at that stream over there, I'm always so thirsty after a night like that, and then, well, then you came along; so you see?"

She raised her beautiful wings up over her head, gave them a little ruffle, preened in her breast feathers for a moment, and then, just as if it was the accidental result of her having raised her wings like that, to shake them out, gave another little flutter and next thing Wittgenstein knew she was sitting next to him on his branch, staring deep into his eyes with her dark, liquid ones, and causing that tingle all over again.

"So, of course, I'll just follow the migration route that my instincts lead me to, wouldn't you think that best?" she said. "In fact, why don't you come along with me? I'm sure my friends would be delighted to meet such a fine-looking chap."

Wittgenstein was dizzy in response to all this attention. He stared back at her, darted a glance at the lace-curtain window across the way, saw the shape of the Professor sitting by the window with a book, looked back at the grosbeak with her slightly ironic twinkle and her eyes like deep pools of water, and said, "How far is it?"

E vening grosbeaks are strong flyers. Wittgenstein would not have stood a chance had it not been for his daily exercise flights as well as his once-a-week or so longer excursions into town and out to the old basswood and along the railway tracks. But even with all that muscle build-up, and the good food and care, he was breathing pretty hard at the end of the first two hours and had to ask her to take a break for a moment. He landed and thirstily licked the dewdrops from the underside of a shady leaf at the edge of a stream, and caught his breath. The grosbeak did not seem to mind this much, although she did have a habit of looking away off into the distance every few seconds. After a while Wittgenstein was ready to go again, and, as it turned out, it was she who called the next pause. "Do you see that box over there?" she said. "Outside that little cabin? Sometimes humans put out boxes like that with some good seeds in them. Unusual in this part of the world, but in the Ohio countryside we see them a lot. Let's go and have a look."

The bird feeder was newly filled. There was cracked corn and millet and barley, and a few large streaked sunflower seeds. The two travellers were hungry, and stayed there for nearly half an hour, flying to a nearby bush every so often to scan the surroundings for any sign of a cat, say, or pigeons. Inside the little house a young woman carrying a baby came to the window and peered out, and called back to a man who was eating his lunch, "My goodness, Charles! There is the strangest-looking grosbeak at the feeder, along with one of those dear evening grosbeaks. Bring the field glasses and have a look."

(Later that evening when farm friends came for a visit and a cup of tea, the young woman, who was very imaginative, unknowingly took the first steps towards building herself a reputation for untruthfulness when she told Farmer Birkenfeld and his wife that she and Charles had discovered a new breed of grosbeak that afternoon.)

As the day wore on Wittgenstein had to stop more and more frequently, and the grosbeak began to show some impatience. "My friends are going to be very cross if we're late," she said once. And then, later, and even snippier, "It's going to be difficult enough to explain to them why I am keeping company with a fancy stranger, but if you can't keep up—I mean we *are* a travelling company, you know, and we do expect everyone to keep up."

When they finally settled for the night by the edge of a marsh they could hear a brace of ducks, out of sight, probably on the water among the dried, pale brown strands and stocks of last year's cattails and arrowhead plant. The drake was complaining about the lack of water plants to eat, and the duck was reminding him that it was just lucky there were no hunters about and that the first lilies would be appearing soon, just be patient.

"And there sure aren't too many seeds around, either," Wittgenstein said wearily. He had knocked around the almost empty heads of some familiar plant stalks at the marsh side, but was too tired to spend more time foraging.

"Oh dear," the grosbeak said softly to herself. "He's having a hard time keeping up."

She went off on her own for a while. Even in the lowering dark she soon found a teaberry plant, right where it should be, under a spread of red oaks, on a sandy bank beside the swamp. She brought him back a couple of the winter-dried red berries, and fed them to him. They were pulpy and spicy, and the aroma made him feel sleepy. As he drifted off he thought she said something like, "My dear colourful friend, it's been great knowing you." But then his head drooped and he was gone for the night. In the morning, when he opened his eyes, she was gone.

For a few minutes, Wittgenstein flapped hopelessly from tree to tree calling out "Hello? Hello?"

But he knew. "What a dope I was," he said with a sigh. "Now let's see. Which way did we come in here? Where do I go to find the railway tracks?"

He had not been paying attention. On the one hand the strain of keeping up with his verdant friend, and on the other the pure tingling excitement of her, had quite caused him to forget about landmarks and directions. He had simply no idea. He had not even been paying attention to where the sun was, which, for a migrant like the grosbeak, is completely unconscious, and sure, and automatic. Yesterday the budgie had found his way back to the house with the lace curtains only by accident, and it was only a ten-minute flight from town. Today he was hours away, hours of fast, heart-pounding flight. He remembered that there was a very large body of water off in the distance, he thought to the right, no, that was earlier, well in fact there had been two—or maybe three? Oh dear. Would he be lucky enough to find those geese somewhere, tending their lakes, and get some navigational advice from them?

"The first thing to do is to find a big lake," he said. "Then perhaps I shall recognize it, and be able to remember where we came from, and then . . ."

But he set off on an entirely wrong heading, due north, in the general direction, though of course he could not know that, of the wilderness park.

Spring brought a turbulence of new life to the wilderness park, and for a few days Astur the Magnificent, formerly of the Royal Court of St. Petersburg, First Position in the Voyeikoff mews, had a full pannell and a restful afternoon almost every day. The woods rang with her sharp cry as she cruised back up from the forest floor with a crumpled furry shape in her claws, moles, squirrels, not as many grouse as she would have liked, and for reasons, some will recall, she was being a little cautious about rabbits. But on the whole, those dreary days at the end of winter were forgotten and her confidence was returning.

Spring is mating time. She was twice approached by young male goshawks, and twice she rebuffed them as being beneath her, too young, too, well, unpolished in their ways. The second of the two was a little larger than most males. The male goshawk is known to falconers as a tiercel, which means "third," because they are about one-third smaller than the female, who is the true hawk, the real hunter. Astur found this fellow comely, but his speech was rough, country speech, and he had no manners.

He was, however, insistent. Two days running he brought her a haunch of rabbit, fresh-killed, as a gift or bribe. The dripping, mangled rabbit flesh was tempting, that was undeniable, and the haunches were big enough to indicate that this fellow was a capable hunter. But perhaps that did not serve his mating intentions very well with this particular goshawk, given her recent experience with a varying hare.

On the third day she had had enough of this fellow. When he came and perched silently before her, his eyes gleaming with admiration and desire, she also sat silent on her perch for a few minutes, staring back at him, and then suddenly roused and screamed, "Begone, or I shall eat you!"

The terrified boy, sensing that she meant it, fled.

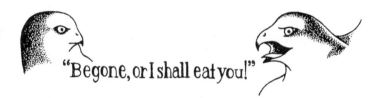

"Begone, or I shall eat you!"

And so the goshawk rested solitary with her pride. We might think it too bad that she would not take a mate here in these Ontario woods, and enrich the goshawk blood-stock with her finely tuned European and Russian genes and chromosomes. And there were times when she sighed with a momentary rush of regret. She was lonely for good talk (and, too, for the calming, affectionate touch of a hand teasing up her mail, and the remembered sound of a young Prince making a soft *gluck, gluck* in his throat, as he stroked her).

But a goshawk is nothing without her pride, and pride won out. The next day, just to prove to herself she could do it, she hunted all the day long and did not try for a single smaller animal — mole or mouse or squirrel — as she was determined to take a fine rabbit and banish the embarrassed memory of that white blob of a snowshoe. It took her three days to find one, but find one she did, another snowshoe rabbit, its spring coat coming on in ragged patches of light brown among the shabby white. She plotted this one perfectly and carried it out meticulously.

The hare had been brought to a stop by the sweet smell of a clump of fresh new wild sorrel that had burst into leaf on a sunny patch of grassy open ground, a long way from his burrow and not very close to ground cover in the forest either. He was intoxicated by the lush taste of this fresh stuff after a long winter of foraging for frozen berries or making do with his stored supply of dried grasses. They are aromatic and nourishing, but you get tired of the same stuff day after day.

So, fresh food for a moment distracted him from his usual wariness. The hawk came at him out of the trees twenty metres away, almost at ground level, faster than a line drive to left that the shortstop could only wave at, and in just as straight a line. The sun was behind her, which is usually good for aerial combat, but it did throw a shadow ahead that whipped the big hare's head around and started him running almost soon enough to save his life. He leapt two metres to the right in a first breathtaking bound, and dug in and cut left again, towards the nearest trees, not near enough, and then right again because the burrow would be safer than the trees, and there was no bramble or low cover in this part of the forest.

The hawk was closing fast, still in the air, no need to hit the ground running in this open territory, no trees to dodge, just try to anticipate which way the now squealing prey would zig or zag the next time. And on about the fourth zig she got it, made her turn at the same moment as his, in the same direction, cut him off at the pass, hurtled against his much bigger body with the advantage of her velocity, and sank one set of razor talons into his neck, just behind the ears, and the other into his left hip. The spine cracked instantly, painlessly. The terrified beast felt nothing. Blackness was immediate, total. After a thudding series of skidding lateral bumps as his body absorbed the impact, the two creatures, locked together, came to a stop against a clump of beaver grass. The hawk stepped calmly back to survey her achievement. She looked around in the clearing for a moment as if to invite applause. She bent to her work.

❧❦❧

*O*ur Wittgenstein, although he has learned a great deal about life in the uncaged world, is not a creature of the wild and can never become one. Clever as he is, he just does not have the built-in, instinctual tools to make it on his own through a world populated by the hunters and the hunted.

Days went by, and turned into weeks. Wittgenstein realized that he had spent most of the summer trying to find some familiar landmark, or water mark, anything to give him some clue as to which way lay the homeward path, and that by now it was really hopeless. The territory was unlike anywhere he had ever been. There was water in every direction: big lakes and small, rivers and streams and swamps, great craggy rocks and tall, whispering pines.

He was very hungry. He came down by the edge of a stream where it curled around the foot of a steep, stone-faced hill. And he paused in a bit of a pool, with a sandy bottom, small trout lazing around, easily seen in the clear slow water, and a large clump of cattails at one side where the loop was widest and the current slowest.

There were four large animals digging at the roots of the cattails, and munching what they brought up. They were big, all right, but they did not look dangerous with their lazy soft eyes and their broad, flat, leathery tails. Wittgenstein clung to the stem of a tall, brown, last year's cattail with its pale furry spike at the top, and looked down at the beavers. They calmly looked up at him, and kept on munching.

"Excuse me," Wittgenstein said. "I am lost and I wonder if you know where the railway tracks are?"

The beaver who seemed the eldest, a black head with some wisps of grey here and there, put down the root he was chewing on, and said, "I think what you mean is what we call the Rolling Thunder. We can hear it at night sometimes. My mother had a very bad experience with it once. It lies a good two days' swim that way." He nodded towards the north.

"But of course, you don't swim, do you. I would suppose that the way you creatures travel, you could be there in a few minutes, I don't know. Fly that way, down this stream till you get to a big river, turn right and keep on going. I hope that helps." The beaver nodded amiably, and then he and his family, one by one, slipped into the water, submerged and disappeared. It was only then that Wittgenstein noticed another beaver resting at the edge of the pond, just out of the water, a big beaver whose fur was entirely white. The white beaver nodded in recognition that he had been seen. Then he said something very strange.

"I think you must be the creature one of my fellow judges spoke about at our meeting two weeks ago," he said. "And I hope your inquiry about the way home indicates that you have paid attention to what he told you. He is very wise.

"For a bird," the white beaver added with a twinkle, and then he too slipped into the water and was gone.

Wittgenstein sat there on the branch thinking about that. What an extraordinary thing. But of course, the owl had said that his fellow judges were not all owls. A white beaver. And the owl had white feathers all over his head.

He pondered this until a considerable amount of time had passed. The sun was slanting low. Wittgenstein came down to the ground and foraged. The season was well on, and there were both new seeds and some wisps of cattail fur with last year's tiny seeds fastened to them high up on the stalks. That was difficult eating because of all the fuzz, and the seeds were very small, but tasty. He kept at it and at last began to feel better in that department. Then he came down to the edge of the pond again, for a drink.

As he lifted his head, the way birds do, to let the water run down his throat, his eye caught the gleam of another eye, a pair of eyes, just sticking up above the surface, shaded by cattail stalks, slit-shaped eyes, with knobbly tops. The eyes rose a little higher, and in front of them a wide, grim mouth also surfaced, just below two nostrils set in a mottled green face, just above a pale white fat rubbery throat that pulsed slowly up and down. It was pretty awful, and Wittgenstein was both frightened and fascinated. He was about to say something polite, by way of making a civilized exit, when a terrible thing happened. It happened so fast that Wittgenstein did not see it coming. A long pink tongue, like a whip with a fat tip, snaked out of the bullfrog's mouth, and wrapped around Wittgenstein's legs, sticking to them with its slimy glue. If Wittgenstein had not had his claws driven firmly into the dead, half submerged branch he was standing on to drink, he would have been whipped back into that wide, thin-lipped devouring machine before anyone could have noticed, supposing anyone were watching. But Wittgenstein was anchored firmly to his branch, and the urgent tug of that tongue, instead of capturing the bird, pulled the frog up and forward in a kind of tumbling lurch. The frog was totally surprised. The last bird he had eaten, a young finch, a good deal smaller than Wittgenstein, had been snapped into the wide mouth in less than a second, and then spent an hour going down into the stomach where it lay digesting for almost a week. Now he was tongue-stuck to a pair of tough little legs locked to a heavy piece of wood, and upside down to boot.

The terrified budgie, not as well equipped as he should have been with instincts and habits to help him out of a fix like this, nonetheless did the one thing that was left for him to do. He lunged at the stretched cord of that terrible, grasping tongue, the long pale thing between him and the fumbling frog who was still trying to get himself back upright, thrashing and throwing up curtains of water. Wittgenstein bit down, hard.

The coiled, gluey terrible thing around his legs went limp. He spread his wings and gave an enormous shove, and pulled loose, and clattered away into the sky, flashing left and then whipping right. How could he know that there was nothing following him? His brain was bursting with terror.

In the meantime, the fat lump of frog in the swamp below was gingerly reeling in the long hawser of that deadly tongue of his, which seemed to have been thoroughly spoiled for any further use, as far as he could tell.

It was getting dark. "High up," Wittgenstein said to himself. "And away from the water."

The sun had set and the spring night was chilly. On a high point of land, a mound looming over the point where the river widened into a lake, there was a dense cluster of big old pines, their branches thickly interlaced. A fortress on a hill, a good safe place for the night. The place smelled funny, a bit fetid. It was too dark to see clearly certain hooded figures hunched on their branches in this pinewood on the top of a hill, dark figures from whom the fetid smell was coming. Wittgenstein was so tired he might not have noticed anyway, even if there had still been a bit of sunlight. But there was not. He settled into a deep hole that a pileated woodpecker had made a few years ago. Somebody else had nested there, he could tell from the feathers and the smells, but it was dry, empty and safe. His heart slowed down. He slept. He had no idea that there were twenty tall brooding figures, each more than forty times his weight and ten times his length, also settling down for the night, all around him.

He awoke in the morning to hear those turkey vultures, for that is what they were, coming to the surface after their night of heavy, well-fed sleep. At first there had been just a general rumble of deep snores, like a carpet of sound. Then the snores began to break up with a few clicks and the odd short-tempered curse. There were remarks about rheumatism, or "This lousy branch, you can't trust white pines any more." Over to one side someone was coughing, a long, rasping cough. "Oh my, I won't last the summer, at this rate." There was some quite unseemly spitting and other disagreeable early morning sounds.

Curious, if a little scared, Wittgenstein crept to the rim of his woodpecker hole to better listen in. He gathered that there was going to be a meeting of some kind, but that the official meeting still had to wait for a cadet branch of the Association, whose members had spent the night on another lake and would join the main assembly presently.

A young female vulture started to boast about a fine garbage pile at a fishing lodge nearby. Another voice said, "Wait till the others are here. I don't want to have to listen to this twice. You know what you are like." Three or four more came humping in for the mid-morning conference, ugly bald red heads punctuated by cruel-looking hooked bills under their sad eyes.

Wittgenstein thought it prudent not to move and attract attention. Although he was hungry, he found the discussion *extremely* interesting. He moved closer to the sill of his woodpecker hole, so that he could hear better.

The conference came to order. The Vulture Party Boss began by complaining that the tributes of carrion the others had brought him were not up to the usual standards. The other vultures rolled their eyes. The Boss always said something like this and nobody took it seriously. Then it was time for regional reports.

The Fishing Resort led off with, "They throw out cheese there. That's what makes it so great," she says eagerly, but another bird says, "What's cheese? It sounds too fresh to me."

"No! No! It's not fresh at all, it's lovely, it's *crawling* with mould, green stinking mould. You can smell it three miles away downwind. Anyway, it's rotten milk to start with, see, but it's solid. You can get your claws into it."

Another says, "That's nothing. I've found a gully where a farmer is throwing away pork guts. There's no people and no bother except when he comes with another load."

"Good and rotten?"

"Well, you have to wait a day or two, sometimes. See, it's fresh when he dumps it there. Disgustingly fresh. If you're not too greedy and let it sit a day or two then it turns green and the maggots start to appear and then you know it's ready to eat."

"Ooh. Maggots. I ate some by mistake once, can you imagine!"

"Alive? You ate something fresh and alive?"

"Ooh. It was an accident. I didn't mean to. It was awful."

"Fresh meat is the most revolting thing I ever heard of," said the Party Boss sternly. "Eating fresh meat. Revolting. Repulsive. Nauseating. Even if it is only insect meat. You should know better than to talk about disgusting things like that when we are discussing gourmet food."

Several older birds nodded and croaked agreement. The Boss went on.

"Listen. Many birds and animals despise us because we eat the dead. A judge, an acquaintance of mine, sort of, he says that even humans despise us for that. Humans! Who provide so much of our food. And the dead things they leave all over the place? Who do they think tidies up their roadways? Oh I know, you think I'm just a party boss holding onto my position till some youngster pushes me off my perch. But, Vultures, we should be proud of what we do. We clean up the planet. Think what it would look like if we weren't out there doing our duty every day. Our duty is our pleasure, of course. But if the other birds—and even those violent, destructive, hateful humans—if my friend the judge is right about that—even they ought to realize that the whole place would be littered with death if it weren't for us and the crows and the ravens. So think about that, Vultures, and go about your days with pride, and understand that you have a great cause."

"We clean up the planet."

There was a clatter of applause. "A noble speech," Wittgenstein heard, and, "Never heard him better. Forget sometimes how wise the old fellow is." The meeting adjourned.

As the sun rose higher in the sky, there was a soft rise of heated air from the hill. The vultures finished their reports on the best eating places, had a brief vote for new directors, and then drew lots as to who would be the outriders on the thermal column. Then the Boss said, "All right, off we go," and they rose heavily into the air, trailing their stink but exhibiting unexpected aerial grace. The two outriders, flapping just on the edges of the thermal, called the others upwind to the centre of the rising column of air, where most of them would not have to flap their wings at all, just glide in a circle There they formed their own living column, thirty or more birds by now. The turkey vulture's wingspread is about two metres, and once they were airborne, and far enough away that they were just black aerial shapes and you could not longer see the cruel wrinkled eyes and the bare red skulls, they looked quite grand. None but the outriders moved any more than a tail feather to fine-tune a turn, or an outer primary to adjust the angle of bank. The thermal drifted off eastward with its burden of carrion eaters. Wittgenstein watched until he was sure he was safe, and then dropped to the ground to look for breakfast.

When he finally found those railway tracks, some days later, his heart sank. They did not look anything like the tracks that might lead him home. They disappeared for long stretches under long overhanging dark pine branches. They followed the banks of rivers and the shores of little lakes, and stretched over bridges or along built-up wedges of stone and gravel that filled the many little dips and valleys in this unfamiliar landscape. There was no town in sight. Wrong tracks. He felt abandoned, lost, homesick, hungry. He wanted to go home. He sensed the movement of the sun around the sky and feared that winter would come. He felt small and incompetent.

He did, however, discover something very interesting. The forest floor, almost everywhere, was littered with cones fallen from the millions of pine and spruce trees. Hopping through the underbrush, looking for some early berries or anything else he might eat, Wittgenstein caught the faint scent of something nutty when he kicked aside one of these cones, an older one whose scales were mostly open at one end, but still tightly shut towards the base. He pecked away at it, tugging loose a few scales, and found that at the base of each scale there was a small, dark seed.

"This is a taste that will take some getting used to," he thought. But as he looked around, at the tens of thousands of cones of varying size and colour, some still sticky and green, others all splayed and broken, he realized that he had stumbled upon an endless supply of food. This was not as good as going home, but it helped him get through the day.

It was this food supply that opened the next chapter in the remarkable young bird's dramatic life, while coming close to shutting down that life for good.

Chapter Three

Crossings

Astur the Magnificent was having a tough time. All through that spring and summer, despite the occasional fine hit like the hare on the clump in the clear, she had noticed herself getting slower, less sure, especially in those low-flying chases close to the ground in the thick woods. Where she had once prided herself on being able to fly through closely packed tree trunks without risking a single primary feather, she now felt reluctant to head into the bush any more deeply than where the trees were at least a wingspread and a half apart, say 130 centimetres. And that was not very deep into most parts of the forest.

There was a stately stand of tall red pine on the top of a bluff (it was on a lake that humans called Red Pine Bay, but of course she did not know that), but it was too open to give cover to the game the goshawk pre-ferred — small rabbits and partridge and other plump, ground-loving birds. She often missed her prey and was uncomfortably lean. Now, this did mean that her digestion was in very good order: she never overate, which a hawk often does in the wild when she does not know where the next meal is coming from. In fact, in most respects the old huntress was in better form than she had any right to be, at the advanced age of fifteen. She was fearfully homesick for the mews. Most nights she dreamed of gleaming strips of Ural beef, cut from the loin. She was hungry all the time.

So one afternoon, when she saw the small, bright spot of varied colours pecking its way among the pine cones on that lovely hill in Red Pine Bay, while the insignificant creature did not look like much more than a mouthful or two, it certainly looked unconcerned, and a bit slow and soft. "An easy take," she said to herself, *une proie facile*, as she sailed in on silent wings and lit without a sound on a dead branch, high up on the west side of the red pines. She looked around carefully, sizing up the territory below, and taking a moment to assure herself of the line of attack and the desirability of the lunch at the end of her swoop. Pretty small, yes. And the Czar knows what it will taste like, we have never seen anything quite so vulgar in all our days except for some of those circus clowns that the Duke used to engage for the young Prince's birthday parties.

She went to rouse, gave herself a little talking-to ("Take your time, Highness: dignity, grace"), and then dropped straight down from the branch, her wings folded, ready to spread when she came within a wing-spread of the ground; to sail straight and true to the target without so much as a flap, she thought, just a feathered guided missile, the wings doing the guiding.

And it was at precisely that moment that the little budgerigar looked up and saw the missile coming. Indignant more than frightened, he hopped sideways onto a trunk, stepped smoothly into an old pileated woodpecker's hole, and screeched at the frustrated goshawk.

"*Espèce d'assassin!*" Wittgenstein yelled. "*Type vulgaire! Regardez là où vous trespassez, sale bête!*"

Which was a series of insults of the very worst order, language that the haughty hunter had never heard addressed to herself, though she had overheard similar vulgarities from the servants in the yard around the mews, but really, but then, well, this was extraordinary. This . . . this ragamuffin coloured thing, this . . . *mountebank* . . . was speaking in French! Vulgar French, to be sure, but beautifully enunciated, and, my God, was he sure of himself.

The goshawk put out her spoilers, braked in the air, extended her landing gear, dropped to the forest floor, looked up to the hole in the bole of the broad old pine where the tiny coloured head could barely be seen, and whispered, largely to herself, "*Regarde-moi ça!*"

"You really ought to look where you're going," the budgie said indignantly, still in French, from within his refuge. "If I hadn't stepped out of the way you might have knocked me down, you big rude thing."

"Rude." That was what he said.

But he said it so beautifully. Such articulation. The goshawk was overcome with nostalgia. She had not heard her language spoken at all for so many years now, and to hear it from a *bird* in this strange foreign land? A bird? And a very odd-looking bird at that. Not so vulgar after all, she guessed, if it could speak so beautifully. Would it speak again? Had she, Astur the Magnificent, possibly misunderstood? Of course she had not. It was unmistakeable. When you hear someone speak in the language you were brought up in, and have not heard since, well, since you were, you know, really *somebody* . . . you forget about being hungry. You forget about your strange surroundings. You just want to have a little chat.

But you do not forget your position in life. She hopped up to a branch a few feet above Wittgenstein's safe house, looked down on him (she always preferred to look down on others), and tried to speak in measured tones.

"I am a goshawk," Astur said, with what she hoped was grace and dignity, although she was still a little out of breath. "And I am meant to hunt and destroy small creatures like yourself. It is my destiny. This is not meant to insult you, I hope you understand. It is simply a law of nature and as an aristocratic person I have great respect for the law.

"As should you," she added, after waiting for a reply that did not come. Wittgenstein was as astonished as the Goshawk had been by his French, to hear a reply in tones even more beautifully modulated than what he was used to from the Professor. "You must understand," she said, "that where I come from . . ."

Unsettled to hear herself talking so freely — Wittgenstein's words had unlocked something inside her — Astur began to talk unrestrainedly. Words poured out of her. All those dreams and longings burst to the surface. Before long she was telling him the story of her life.

She had just reached the part where they boarded the ship for New York, when her eye caught a small movement, off to the left, towards the river on the west side of the hill of red pines. It was a rabbit, a plump, careless male, who had just hopped into view and was calmly nibbling on the rich grasses that grew in the open sun there, a hundred feet from the edge of the woods. There was no shelter behind him, only the steep slope down to the water. He would not be likely to run for cover in the woods, for it was from the woods that his fate was about to emerge at the speed of a meteor. In mid-sentence the goshawk paused in her narration. Her head swivelled slowly towards the rabbit as she gauged the distance.

"Please go on," Wittgenstein said, after a second or so, as the hawk's dark eyes narrowed on her prey out there on the sunny grass.

"I . . . I may have to leave you for . . . a moment," the goshawk said. "I will be happy to finish the story . . . after I . . ."

The careless rabbit had turned his back on the woods and was sniffing the wind that flowed across the river from the west bank. Perhaps if the wind had not been as fresh as it was he might have heard the wings propelling that feathered projectile straight at him, out of the woods, with its eight razor-like claws extended for the kill. He leapt in the air a fraction of a second too late. The attacker was still a metre above the ground, and the rabbit's panicky leap put him directly in front of her, still in mid-air at the moment of impact. The claws sank deep, one set at the neck, the other at the flank. It was over in less than a second. Wittgenstein gaped, amazed, grateful for the safety of his hole in the tree. The hawk dined well.

It was some time before she returned, carefully cleaning her beak and her claws. Wittgenstein sank back out of sight.

"It is quite safe, little colourful. I will not need to eat you or anything else for at least a day or two now. And indeed, I would rather talk with you than eat you. You have no idea how much I am enjoying our discussion."

This was strange, as the budgie had said almost nothing since his first outburst that had stopped the goshawk in mid attack. She had done all the talking. But she was calmer now, even a little sleepy after her substantial lunch. Lunch does that to older creatures. And arrogant as she was, she had been taught the basic courtesies and now recognized that she had not given her new acquaintance the floor for even a moment. It was time to do that.

"Perhaps you could tell me *your* story," she said after a moment.

"Well, all right," Wittgenstein said, and before long things were pouring out of him, as well.

He spoke of the Professor with great affection. He left out the part about the cage, and just told about the good food and the long talks at night, and the warm house. Sleepy though she was, the Goshawk listened with attention. Wittgenstein's account of life at home made the Professor's house sound like a palace. "I don't know why you left," the hawk said. "It sounds very lovely."

"I flew too far one day and got lost," the budgie said. "Well, I was having an adventure with a lady, to be truthful. But I am sorry now. I would really like to go home but I don't know how to find my way."

"You flew too close to the sun," said the goshawk, who was educated.

Astur the Magnificent sighed nostalgically. She flipped lazily up on to a higher branch, folded her wings, settled, and said softly "I shall just have a short sleep now. Please don't be afraid of me any more. I am beginning to have an idea. About how we might, ah . . . well, I shall tell you about it after I . . ."

Her voice trailed off. The powerful dark eyes faded and shut. She was sound asleep.

Wittgenstein thought it best to stay put. He was asleep himself when a voice just outside his shelter woke him. An hour had gone by.

"I wish to speak," said the goshawk. Wittgenstein waited. After a while she went on.

"Do you suppose," the hawk said, "do you suppose that if we flew very high, right up to where the clouds are, and I used my very powerful eyes to scan in all directions . . . Do you suppose that we might see some land that resembles the land you came from, and perhaps find our way there?"

It seemed an unlikely idea to the little bird. "Besides, I tried flying up to the clouds once, and I could never get there. I'm just not up to it."

"I could carry you with me." She raised one foot, curled it around a hanging pine cone with a gentleness that surprised Wittgenstein (having watched those claws at the work they were designed for), and lifted the cone away from its twig without so much as bending even one of its little scales.

"I am quite used to carrying things as I fly," she said.

"Even small birds," she added, with an unseemly giggle.

Now, a large dog like a retriever or an Alsatian will carry a kitten around the house cradled gently in its mouth, the kitten looking up and even picking bits of stuff out from between the teeth of the big hunter. Those teeth are so powerful they could easily break the neck of a cat twenty times the size of a kitten, a lynx, say, maybe even an ocelot. In the same way the raptor's powerful feet were sensitive as well as strong, able to pick tiny insects out of her

"I am quite used to carrying things as I fly."

feathers as she preened. They were wise feet. She is known in the old hunting literature as a "beast of the foot" because it is those claws that undertake her most important economic activity. So the goshawk knew that she could easily and gently carry her new friend a mile high in the sky, if he would trust her. And there was such earnestness in her way of suggesting that they might . . . *go home together* . . . and such a powerful tugging towards home in his little heartstrings, that the little bird thought, "Why not? I'd only die out here anyway, when winter comes. I am very lonely. She *says* she will be my friend. She seems very proud and very difficult. But I don't think she is untruthful. And what have I got to lose?"

Try to see the strange picture. It will be easier if you have been in a house when one of those dogs carries around a kitten or a baby raccoon, in the jaws that could crack a skull. But it is still a strange picture. More than two thousand metres above the treetops, with the lakes way down below glistening like beads on the string of rivers that join them, a tiny speck seen from the ground is really a great-winged hunting bird who is carrying a small friend so gently in those curved talons — and at the same time so securely — that he could probably stop clinging to the middle toe of the goshawk's talons, to keep the rush of air from blowing him away, clinging as if he were on a pine branch in a windstorm. But he clings hard all the same, and tries to scan out the long curve of the world below, but his eyes are watering in the rush of cold early September air, very cold at that altitude, and he can't see very much at all.

"To the north, away from the sun, there is nothing but lakes and forest," Astur tells him. "So I do not think it could be that way. Do you agree?" The budgie agrees.

"Far to the west there is a great water that goes to the horizon and then disappears. It could be the ocean I crossed on that ship with my prince so many years ago, but I do not think so, it is in the wrong direction though it looks just as big." (She was looking at the edge of the spreading Georgian Bay.) "To the east, more lakes and forest. But to the south, beyond another big lake, I can see open fields and — I think — some places where humans live, some buildings, although it is too far to be sure."

Wittgenstein's heart is now beating very rapidly, and not just from the altitude. This sounds very exciting. Just by going up so high she has — just possibly — found something that he has been dreaming of, but could never have seen from the ground. "Could we go in that direction?" he says quietly.

His Highness Prince Vasily Voyeikoff

^c/o Major General His Excellency Sascha Count Ivanov

321 Houston Street East, 3rd Floor, Apartment 12b

New York, New York. USA

Your Highness:

I understand from a journalist friend of mine, who
met you recently in New York, that you are one of a
number of distinguished subjects of the late Czar of All
the Russias, his Majesty Nicholas of sainted memory,
who have been forced to leave your homeland as a
result of certain unhappy events in that country.

As a student and a professor of language, I am in the
process of developing what I believe to be my life
work, a study of the origins of language in the human
brain, and the social and physical conditions that shape
various tongues as they are spoken around the globe.

I am very much interested in the special character of
the French language as reportedly spoken in the Court
of St. Petersburg, your home. I write to ask if you would

consider visiting me, as my guest, in my most modest circumstances, in order that we may have a written record of that most interesting linguistic development while there are still people alive who experienced it.

There are regular trains from your city to Toronto, and connections from Toronto three times a day to a nearby town, where I would be pleased to meet you with my new motor car.

It is understood without saying that financial considerations would be of no concern to a great gentleman such as yourself, but my grant from the Royal Society, for this work, is sufficient for me to insist—<u>as a matter of honour</u>—that I take responsibility for the costs entailed in such a journey.

Yours very truly,

Henry Harley

Henry Harley, B.A., M.A. Ph. D., D. Litt, D. Sc., FRSC.
General Delivery, Creemore, Ontario
Canada
21 August, 1922

(Original in French)

It had been well on in an early September afternoon before they began the journey, this unlikely pair. So when they came to the shore of a big water—well, the hawk reported that she could see a collection of dwellings on the far shore, but the budgie's eyes could not quite make it out—anyway, when they came to that shore, and the sun was setting very red beyond the town Astur could just make out, it seemed like a good place to rest for the night.

"Well, my goodness!" Wittgenstein said. "My goodness, I don't think there is another budgie in the world who's had a trip like that!"

"Were you comfortable? I didn't hold you too hard?"

"There were a couple of moments," said the budgie, "when I thought you might have forgotten, ah, what I was for. And then you seemed to remember."

The night came down upon them gently. The hawk was still digesting her rabbit, and so she was ready for a good long sleep. Wittgenstein was too excited to sleep easily. It was well after midnight, and a pale half moon rising in the east, before he finally closed his eyes.

They were ready to go again by the time the sun came up. Wittgenstein had found some fat green milk-weed pods at the edge of a small field, and ripped them open and pulled the wet seeds away from the sticky, close-packed silk inside, and had a good feed. The goshawk cast what was left of yesterday's rabbit fur and a few bones, and spent a quiet half hour preen-ing meticulously. As they left the shelter of the hard-wood stand where they had spent the night a pair of young Hungarian partridges scuttled away beneath them, and the hawk was tempted for a moment. But she was not really hungry, and her curiosity about home — even though it was only Wittgenstein's home — was, for now, stronger than her hunting instincts. They set out, due west in the hazy morning, until Astur could see sunlight reflecting from windows in a town across the bay, and headed that way, because the budgie had spoken of a town.

A white boat, fat and round with a black smoke-stack pouring out black smoke, was heading towards them from the town's harbour. The boat was about halfway across the bay and had just turned to head north as the two birds came over it. If the birds had been able to read they would have seen the words THE MIDLAND CITY around her wheelhouse in very big letters, and across her stern and along her bows as well. The decks were packed with people going on a last vacation in the last long weekend of the summer. In the crowd were a man and a woman who carried long binoculars and big linen bags with small books about birds in them. They both saw the goshawk, cruising fairly low now to take a look at this funny fat floating thing crawling with humans, and they both swung their binoculars up towards her.

"My God, Graeme!" the woman said. "It's carrying its prey. Why do you suppose it's carrying its prey, away out here? What is it, anyway?"

"Get the book out, Peggy. Get the hawk section. I would have said it was a goshawk but not away out here. Anyway it's far too big for a goshawk. I'll bet it's an immature bald eagle, that's what it is, and it's got a, uhmm, well I can't make out the dead thing it's carrying, probably a pigeon with its belly ripped open, you can see the red streaks. I think. Boy! Wait till we tell them at the club!"

The boat passed by, and soon the little town with its harbour full of sailboats swam up beneath them. It was not the right town, but the landscape around it—except for the lack of big hills—was *something* like home, and made Wittgenstein feel that they were on the right track. Astur started the long climb to altitude, for another major survey. She was heavier than usual, with her passenger and the remains of the meal that was still working its way through her lower parts. So the climb was slow, but steady, in wide circles, until she was high enough to see for miles in all directions.

It all looked the same, except to the north where it was all water. Not far away there were long stretches of sand beach, dozens of kilometres long and already spotted with the tanned bodies of swimmers and sunbathers.

"I don't know, really," Wittgenstein said, "but something tells me we should go that way," and he looked towards the south. They flew low along those long pale beaches, with the breakers rolling in from the west. Hundreds of people saw the handsome hawk and stopped what they were doing to watch her graceful flight. A few children noticed she was carrying something. At the far end of those beaches, with all the water behind them now and the Goshawk ready for a rest (she had been flying non-stop for almost two hours), they came to another stand of hardwoods, maple and beech, on the outskirts of another small town. "This town is not it either," Wittgenstein said. "But I'm pretty sure I flew over this place that day so long ago, you know? With my yellow and green lady friend with the big beak. I really am pretty sure." He was getting very excited. He was a little cross about Astur needing to stop.

After half an hour's rest she took off laboriously and climbed again for one more major survey, and even before she was half-way to her planned altitude, her little passenger said, "Look at the hills. *Look at the hills!*"

"Look at the hills. Look at the hills!"

❦

Professor Henry Harley
General Delivery, Creemore, Ontario
Canada

Distinguished Schollar:

It is so very kind of you for inviting me to the Canada.

As it happens I have been invited by the directors of my company here at New York to be taking a vacation, as my responsabilties has been very grate for some time and therefore I am free to visit at you for this most interesting project that you have written about.

Therefore I am arriving on the Saturday of the Labouring Days weekend as you proposed. I am looking forward to meeting you at the trainway station at the Creemore city. It will be easy to recognize me as I have a gold monocle which I will wear in my eye to see you.

Yours faithfully

A. R. I. V. Szolzhe-Voyeikoff
September 1st

Post Scriptum: I would, of course, insisting on my bankers dealing with the monetarily aspect, but for my family and me the question of honour that you raised is the supreme of questions, and therefore for that reasons only I am accepting what you insist upon.

A.R.I.V.S-P.

"That is it!" Wittgenstein called up to his wing-beating friend, as they pushed steadily south-ward. "See the tracks? See where they go by the town? Follow those tracks. See the old tin roof building there? It is too bad you don't eat bread, they throw out wonderful crumbs. You could eat some of the pigeons, couldn't you? That would be a service to us all."

"Pigeons are disgusting," the goshawk said. "All fluff and dust. Too much work for what you get."

And then, a few minutes past town, they saw a house with lace curtains. Wittgenstein said they had better stop and perch for a minute in a certain neighbouring maple tree, so that he could collect himself.

∽⟨⟩∾

The man who stepped off the train at the Creemore station that same afternoon was, indeed, wearing a fine gold monocle in his left eye, although there was not any glass in the monocle, it having broken some time ago. The man's suit was of the finest cut of rich Irish broadcloth, although it was grievously worn at the knees, elbows and cuffs. His shoes, while polished to a brilliant shine, were also badly worn. Henry Harley bowed, very correctly. "*Votre Altesse,*" he said. The young man smiled a real smile of pleasure.

"*Cher Professeur,*" he said.

They chatted away in French, cheerfully ignoring poor Vasily's dilapidated clothes and scuffed suitcase. "Ah," said the young man, "these woods remind me so much of home, and the smell of the air. New York is all smoke, you know, smoke and crowds. And this begins to feel like my beloved Russia. It reminds me so much of Astur." And for the rest of the drive out to the little house with the lace curtains, in the Professor's shiny new Hupmobile with its bright-yellow paint and cream-coloured tires Vasily talked of home. The car's roof was down, the day was sunny, the young aristocrat's embarrassment at being fired from his doorman's job at the Waldorf was forgotten. He was, for the first time in years, being treated with the courtesy and humbleness he properly deserved, and by a great scholar.

They pulled in at the house with the lace curtains, and got down from the car. "And where is *your* house?" asked Prince Vasily politely, recovering in time to turn it into a joke, although they both knew that he had made a mistake.

In the airy upstairs room, the sun was beating in just a little too hotly, and so the Professor pulled the lace curtains shut, and poured tea. He was outlining the scope of his project, and beaming with pleasure at his aristocratic guest. The young man was really very bright despite having been raised as a pampered prince. He even seemed to grasp the concept.

It was a complicated concept, and a daring one, suggesting the human capacity for language was built into the very physical structure of the brain, and that all languages around the world were basically built of the same kind of mental building blocks. Henry Harley was away ahead of his time. His ideas, alas, had already been mocked by some of his fellow professors, would be laughed at again when he published them, and would not be taken seriously for another sixty years. But that is another story. For now, both he and his guest were throwing ideas back and forth at dazzling speed.

"So, if I understand you," said the young Prince, "when my peasant-born gatekeeper tells me '*Nyet nichivo ni vazmozhna,*' and my royal grandmother tells me '*Rien n'est impossible,*' and my poor father, who insisted on speaking English in the mews, told me when I was on the verge of giving up on training my Astur, that 'Nothing is impossible,' do you mean that they were all using the same part of the brain to do the same job?"

"Exactly," said Henry Harley, so pleased to be taken seriously.

"Ah," said the Prince. He was now sad at the memory of home, and of his boyhood and his lost goshawk.

There was a soft tapping at the window. Henry Harley did not notice. He had launched eagerly into the next part of the theory. The tapping became louder. "Excuse me," said the Prince. "There appears to be, ah . . ."

A small grainy voice, a soft, precise, husky voice, seemed to be saying through the glass, *"La liberté de la parole est la première liberté."*

Henry Harley heard that. He had been paying attention to the teapot for the moment, and misunderstood the source of that soft voice. "It's funny you should say that," he replied to the Prince, over his shoulder, "I had a pet bird who used to say it, only in English. You sounded just like him for a . . . Oh my goodness. Wittgenstein!"

He rushed to the window and threw it open. A small, tired budgerigar stood on the sill, looking very happy.

"Wittgenstein," Henry Harley said again. The budgie looked to one side. He cocked his head in an inviting kind of a way. A tall shadow moved into view, from where it had been concealed by the edge of the window frame it bent its noble head and looked piercingly into the darker space of the room with its powerful dark eyes. "God be praised," said the Prince in a faint whisper.

The hawk stepped softly across the sill. With one small push of her graceful sails she was sitting on the Prince's sleeve, trying not to pierce the thin cloth, although she was really too excited to think very clearly, and in fact drew a few points of blood before she calmed down. *"Dieu soit loué,"* said the Prince softly, again, not minding the wounds.

"Wittgenstein."   "God be praised."

❧⟡❧

H enry Harley found his guest a suitable job at a hunting lodge, just a few miles away up on the Bay. The owner of the lodge soon had an idea. It was exciting to be able to offer his guests the services of a guide and expert hunter of genuinely royal blood,

138

however unimportant that particular royalty had become in these difficult revolutionary days. And the guy was also a master falconer. What if they acquired a few more trained hawks, and offered the guests some instruction in the rudiments of falconry, and even some genuine hunting of small game with the birds? Vasily knew that he had found home again. And, in the winter it was as cold as St. Petersburg, and the snow fell just as thickly.

The Professor finished his book on language. Kit, the lady journalist, forgiven, came back to Creemore and wrote a fine article about the Professor, for the still-young national publication called *Macleans Magazine*, which had just begun to do feature articles on outstanding Canadians in many fields. The Professor became famous even though his former colleagues at the university said that he was, well, a bit nuts.

He also came to feel that solitude, while good for scholarship, is perhaps not good for all of the wants in life, and invited Kit the lady journalist to consider a different way of being in the world. But there was thirty years' difference between their ages, after all. And Kit had to admit that she had been thinking of looking up the Russian prince, whom she had taken quite a fancy to when they were chatting away on the sidewalk outside the Waldorf-Astoria Hotel. To his credit the Professor saw some good in this, and told her where to find the newly engaged Hunt Director at the lodge.

One day Henry Harley took the train all the way to the city and back in the same day, bringing with him a shy but strong-minded lady budgerigar. This newcomer took her time warming up to Wittgenstein, but within a couple of months was learning to speak French too, which was a start.

A tradition soon established itself. On Christmas, Easter, and on Labour Day (but these were the fixed and unmoveable feasts — there were other long weekends and evenings and birthdays), the newly established hunting guide and professional falconer, whom people at the Lodge were calling Val Piano, would come to visit at the little house with the lace curtains. Everybody there called him Your Highness, just for fun, and took care to help him keep his French in good condition. He would always bring with him his new wife. She was a little older than he, and seemed to be very much in love. She had given up journalism, and was busy writing eccentric and successful novels based on her career as a pioneer woman journalist. Val Piano also brought along a dignified and somewhat frail goshawk. The handsome old bird by then needed a lot of naps, not just in the afternoon. Still, almost every day during these visits, if the weather was clement, she would fly out to a certain local maple tree to perch for half an hour with her old friend and chat about the old days.

During these visits, from time to time Wittgenstein had to stop Astur from rousing at some of the local small birds, especially at one very saucy, vulgar ragged old black rack of disorderly feathers who had bad breath and bad grammar and teased the two of them in an outrageous way. But Wittgenstein's worry about the goshawk's rousing was exaggerated as she had become very slow and quite dependent upon the lovely slips of moosemeat and venison that Val Piano supplied her with. She probably couldn't have hurt even a starling.

But she was still magnificent, for all that.

EPILOGUE

Twelve years have gone by. In a cozy cabin by the lake, on the edge of a wooded property owned by the hunting lodge, a woman in early middle age, wearing rimless spectacles and wearing her hair in a bun, is bent over a notebook on the broad pine kitchen table, writing in pencil by the light of a coal oil lamp. From time to time she lifts her head and glances outside at a lighted window in a neighbouring log cabin, which has been converted into a small mews. There are now six different birds of prey in the mews, including a gyrfalcon, in various stages of their training. Although the woman cannot see it from where she sits, there is a small brass plaque over the door of this cabin on which is inscribed:

THE HOUSE OF ASTUR

On the ground a few metres away from the building are two small mounds in the earth marked by a small granite headstone with:

ASTUR THE MAGNIFICENT

Chiselled into its polished surface, and the dates 1907–1924, and below that the words:

WITTGENSTEIN, HER FRIEND

From time to time the woman looks up from her work, and out to her left, where she can see two figures through the small window of the mews—a man bending over and a boy looking up.

If she could hear them she would hear the man saying, "Do you think you are patient enough to stay with this? If you are really going to train this bird yourself, you might want, at the start, to spend a few nights with her in the mews, and be prepared to get up and speak softly to her if you hear her moving on the block at night."

Even though she cannot hear the words, she can make out the boy's gloved hand as it comes up slowly, behind the small, just fledged, chick of a goshawk, moves softly in towards the back of the bird's legs, and presses against them. The hawklet has no choice. At the light pressure from behind, she raises one foot and then the other, and steps back onto the glove. Now, slowly, gently, the boy brings up his other hand, the index finger crooked, until the knuckle touches her mail. The hawklet looks coolly down at the boy's finger. She bends her head and lowers her already powerful beak towards it. The father's face looks concerned, but he does not intervene. The beak opens. It surrounds the crooked right index finger. It nibbles gently.

From the cabin the boy's mother cannot hear what it is her son is saying as he looks up at his father, but she can tell that his eyes are shining.

THE END